Robert gave a mock sigh.

'Maligned, I am. I thought I'd actually been the perfect boss.'

Frankie chuckled. 'Of course. I expect you're really very kind under that grim and forbidding exterior.'

His eyes flew open and he studied her in genuine astonishment. 'Grim and forbidding? Really?'

She relented. 'No, not really. Mostly you're quite civilised. You only bite if I'm particularly stupid or you're particularly hungry.'

It was an unfortunate choice of words. Something flared in his eyes, and Frankie felt the heat scorch her cheeks.

Kids. . .one of life's joys, one of life's treasures.

Kisses. . .of warmth, kisses of passion, kisses from mothers and kisses from lovers.

In *Kids & Kisses*. . .every story has it all.

Caroline Anderson's nursing career was brought to an abrupt halt by a back injury, but her interest in medical things led her to work first as a medical secretary, and then, after completing her teacher training, as a lecturer in Medical Office Practice to trainee medical secretaries. She lives in rural Suffolk, with her husband, two daughters, mother and assorted animals.

Recent titles by the same author:

THAT'S MY BABY!
A FAMILIAR STRANGER
LOVE WITHOUT MEASURE
TAKEN FOR GRANTED
ANYONE CAN DREAM

AND DAUGHTER MAKES THREE

BY
CAROLINE ANDERSON

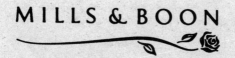

MILLS & BOON

*MILLS & BOON, the Rose Device and
LOVE ON CALL are trademarks of the publisher.
Harlequin Mills & Boon Limited,
Eton House, 18-24 Paradise Road, Richmond, Surrey TW9 1SR*

© Caroline Anderson 1996

ISBN 0 263 79496 2

*Set in Times 10 on 11 pt. by
Rowland Phototypesetting Limited
Bury St Edmunds, Suffolk*

03-9603-48694

*Made and printed in Great Britain
Cover illustration by Simon Bishop*

CHAPTER ONE

'You aren't taking this interview seriously, are you?'

Robert blinked in astonishment. 'I beg your pardon?'

The girl sighed and rammed the long fingers of her right hand through once tidy mousy hair. Well, not really mousy. There were actually some rather beautiful gold lights lurking in it, he noted absently, just waiting for a stray sunbeam to bring them to life—

'I'm just your statutory woman interviewee, aren't I? Why can't you admit it? I'm only here because you have to appear unbiased, but I can tell by your questions that you think I should be curled up somewhere behind a desk chatting to pregnant mothers and peering down children's throats!'

Robert shifted uncomfortably and cleared his throat, embarrassed at being so easily read by the young woman in front of him.

'Not at all,' he demurred, but her fine dark brows shot up sceptically and he sighed. 'All right, perhaps a little. I've got nothing against women doctors; I think they're a necessary—'

'Evil?' she supplied helpfully.

He sighed. 'I was going to say balance. The problem isn't so much your gender as your physique. Orthopaedic surgery is physically demanding—'

'So is general practice. The point is, I don't want to do general practice, I want to do orthopaedics, and I want you to give me the chance.'

Stubborn little cuss. Robert eyed her with fresh interest. 'So what makes you think you'd be any good?'

'I can spot fractures on X-ray plates that other people miss—'

'So you can diagnose. But can you treat those fractures? Have you got the strength to reduce them, to realign the bones and reduce dislocations?' He studied the slender hands lying on the edge of the desk, palms down, the long, fine fingers outspread as if she was ready to spring up and dash off. 'Look at your hands. I doubt if you could even wring a chicken's neck.'

She smiled wryly. 'I doubt if I could, but that's probably because I'm vegetarian and nothing to do with brute force and ignorance.'

'I never mentioned ignorance.'

'You didn't mention skill, either. Or patience and persistence. You need those too, and on that score I'm definitely your man—so to speak.'

Robert was beginning to think that her patience and persistence would be the death of him. 'What evidence have you got to support that extravagant claim?' he asked drily.

'I can do jigsaws,' she told him.

His jaw sagged slightly. Jigsaws? She could do jigsaws? He could play badminton, but it was hardly relevant—

'You know, the double-sided baked bean variety that nobody has the patience for? I don't give up. I persist until whatever I'm doing is done to my satisfaction. I'm a perfectionist, but I know how to compromise. I'm strong, I'm fit and I'm prepared to go to any lengths to do the job well. I won't let you down.'

'Won't', please note, not wouldn't, he thought wearily. As if he'd offered her the job.

'It's physically punishing,' he warned. 'Long hours in Theatre, bending over shattered limbs, piecing them together—'

'Like jigsaws. Exactly.'

'Can you bang a nail in straight? Saw straight? Drill and screw with total accuracy?'

'Yes,' she said. Just like that, without any hesitation.

'Yes?' he pushed.

'Yes. I've been practising. My brother's got a Victorian house. I've been helping him do it up. I'm a dab hand with an electric drill, and I can hammer and chisel and paint in straight lines—'

'How useful,' he said drily.

'Well, if I can paint in straight lines I can cut in straight lines, which might be relevant, I suppose?' she replied, just as drily.

He sighed. 'Look, Ms—'

'Bradley. Frances—Frankie, for preference—and it's Miss but Dr will do. Please, Mr Ryder, give me a chance. I won't let you down.'

'Won't' again. Damn her. He rammed his own fingers through his own hair and sighed again. 'Look, Dr Bradley, I won't lie to you. I've seen another applicant who looks ideal—'

'A man?'

Robert groaned inwardly. 'As it happens. As I was saying, I've seen him, he's right for the job, and I was simply waiting until I'd interviewed you to offer it to him. He's got more surgical experience than you—'

'I can learn. I loved my time in surgery—check my references. I was good at it.'

'Slow, it says. Good, but slow.'

She swallowed, but, damn her, she didn't give up. 'That's because I'm thorough. The SR I was working with missed a thrombosis in a mesenteric artery, and the patient would have died if I hadn't pointed it out. He'd just removed her perfectly healthy appendix and said that must be the trouble, and some people didn't know what pain was. He was so busy flirting with the scrub nurse they could have sewn up the rest of the

surgical team inside the woman and not noticed. A
loop of necrotic bowel was far too subtle!'

He bent over her references again, cupping his chin
in his hand and using his fingers to cover the little
smile that wouldn't be suppressed.

'What if I gave you the chance and you couldn't do
the job in the end?'

'You'd face that possibility with anyone,' she said
fairly. 'I was good on fractures in my time in A and
E, and God knows I saw enough of them. It frustrated
me to bits not to be able to follow them up to Theatre
and finish the job. What if you got someone whose
only asset was his strength? What about the jigsaws?'

He looked up at her again and her eyes trapped his,
mesmerising him. He cleared his throat and tried again.
'As you haven't met the other applicant I can't see
how you can make that judgement—'

'I'm not making any judgements, just putting
forward for instances.' She leant towards him, resting
on those long, elegant fingers, her energy vibrating in
her voice. 'Look, I'm prepared to do it on a trial basis.
If you give me three months, I'll do everything I can
to justify your faith in me.'

He stared at her in amazement. 'You're prepared
to do it on a trial basis?' he repeated, unable to believe
the brass neck of the woman. 'You want me to turn
away a perfectly good applicant so I can give you a
trial?' He was stunned. Justify his faith, indeed! What
faith? He had no faith in her, none at all!

She surged to her feet, nearly six feet of willowy,
tormenting woman, and paced to the window. She was
so slender he could have snapped her in half with
his bare hands, he thought disgustedly. How did she
imagine she could cope?

The sunshine caught her hair and for a moment she
looked like an angel, the gold strands surrounding her

enthusiastic, lovely face like a shimmering halo. Then she turned, a coil of energy that made him feel exhausted just to watch her, and came back to the desk, bracing those beautiful, slender hands on it and leaning towards him, her eyes earnest.

'That's right. It will give us both long enough to see if it could work. If it doesn't, then I'll give up and go quietly.'

He couldn't stop the little snort. The very idea of this young woman giving up and going anywhere quietly was laughable.

She jerked up straight and glared down at him. 'You don't believe me, do you?'

He met her eyes, serious now. The last time he had believed a woman had been his wedding day. He wouldn't make that mistake again.

'Why should I?'

'Because I'm honest. I'll try, and try hard. If it doesn't work, I'll admit it. What I won't accept is not being given a chance just because you think I won't stick at it or won't be strong enough to do it.'

'And will you?'

'Of course. Give me your hand.'

Warily, a little bemused, he held out his hand and her warm, slender fingers curled softly round it and gripped with surprising strength. She settled herself into the chair again, said, 'Ready?' and at his nod he felt the power in her arm challenge his own strength.

She wanted to arm-wrestle? Far be it from him to spoil her fun, but he didn't believe in hurting women—

'Damn! How did you do that?'

She laughed. 'You weren't taking me seriously. You keep doing that, don't you?' She shook her head and laughed again. 'Big mistake.'

He didn't doubt it for a minute! He extricated his hand from her warm and enticing grip and leant back in the chair, regarding her steadily.

'I let you win,' he lied.

She snorted. 'Fiddlesticks. You underestimated me, Mr Ryder. My point is this—I'm strong. I take care of myself—probably better than you do. I won't let you down—I promise.'

Her eyes were grey, not the blue-grey of his but a soft, slightly greeny grey, wide and clear, and they locked with his and wouldn't let go. He could still feel the strength of her grip, the warmth of her hand and he was achingly aware of the soft rise and fall of her very feminine curves under her fine wool sweater as she waited for his answer.

'Please?' she coaxed, and her voice whispered over his senses and did unbidden things to his normally ordered mind.

He felt himself crumble under that misty gaze, and the rigid set of his shoulders sagged slightly under the weight of his foolishness. 'I'll probably regret it,' he found himself saying, 'but yes, Dr Bradley, I'll give you your chance.'

For a moment he thought she was going to jump over the desk and hug him, but with a massive effort she pulled herself together and smiled, and the smile set off little fires in her eyes that warmed the cold recesses of his heart.

'Thank you,' she said, with commendable control, and leant against the chair-back as if sheer will-power had been holding her up. 'So—when do I start?'

He shuffled paper on his desk, still unable to believe what he had done. Was he quite mad? 'The beginning of January? I'll get my secretary to sort out all the details of your salary and so on—she might be able to help you with accommodation as well.'

He pushed his chair back and rose to his feet, going round the desk to usher her out, and as she stood and smiled at him with her megawatt smile a shock of heat coursed through his body.

He crushed it ruthlessly and forced a smile. 'Welcome to the team, Dr Bradley. I'll see you in the new year.'

Her eyes were dancing and a subtle hint of perfume, sensuous and filled with promise, drifted over him as she moved. 'Thank you. I'll look forward to it. Happy Christmas.'

'Thank you. And to you.'

Her strong, warm fingers curled round his again, familiar now and somehow enticing, and with a mumbled goodbye he closed the door behind her and leant against it with a groan, grateful for the long white coat which disguised his body's betrayal.

A knot of tension gripped his chest and he rubbed it absently. What had he done?

Ah, well, it was only three months. Hopefully he could survive.

He wasn't convinced. Her perfume lingered on the air, conjuring a memory of her smiling eyes and soft, lush figure. Frances Bradley, he realised with a sinking feeling in his gut, was one complication he could frankly have done without. . .

She found him in the sister's office, dressed in green theatre pyjamas, his feet, in white anti-static boots, up on the desk, a file open on his lap. The remains of a cup of coffee lurked beside him, and she could see by his shadowed jaw that he had been up all night.

He looked forbidding and rather cross, she thought, and her heart sank. Oh, well, it was all her own fault, and if he proved a pig to work with she had only herself to blame. After all, he hadn't wanted her.

Frankie approached him cautiously.

'Happy New Year,' she ventured.

He lifted his head and stared at her, then gave a tiny snort of disbelief. 'Is it?'

'I hope so. So, what's on the menu today?' she said brightly.

Robert Ryder scowled, his blue-grey eyes as chilly as the January wind that sliced across the Suffolk countryside. 'Emergency theatre work, mainly. Several casualties after last night's festive stupidity—I thought you weren't coming in until tomorrow? It's a bank holiday today.'

She shrugged and smiled. 'Thought I'd come and find out where everything was, see if I could help.'

She could see he wasn't convinced. The scowl lurked in the back of his eyes, and her heart sank even further.

'It's all under control,' he said shortly, snapping the file shut. 'You should have stayed in bed while the going was good.'

'It wasn't that good—the bed. Cold and lumpy, really. Most unappealing. It was no hardship to get out of it.'

His scowl worsened. Oh, damn, she thought, he regretted his impulse. She stifled the sigh and let her smile slip a little. 'Well, then, if there's nothing else I can do, do you mind if I watch you operate?'

He shrugged his broad shoulders slightly, and a cynical little smile touched his lips. 'Oh, I think you can scrub—you never know, I might find a use for you since you're here. We might as well find out sooner rather than later if you aren't going to be able to cope.'

Oh, hell. Frankie dredged up a smile. 'Oh, I'll cope, Mr Ryder; don't you worry.'

'I'm not worried, Dr Bradley—just unconvinced.'

'Then give me a chance to convince you. What's the first case?'

He dropped his feet to the floor and stood up, stretching wearily and kneading the back of his neck with one large, long-fingered hand. 'Here.' He snapped some X-rays up onto the light box and stood back. 'What can you tell me about this?'

'Ouch,' she murmured.

'Would you care to be more specific?' he said drily.

'Sure.' She pointed to the radiograph of the right thigh and indicated a long, diagonal fracture of the shaft of the femur. 'This, obviously, and also here.' She moved her finger up to the femoral neck, where it angled across to the pelvis. 'There's a slightly impacted fracture here, and the hip joint's gone on the other side, I think,' she murmured, looking at the other plate of the left side. She peered more closely at it, and frowned. 'Is there another view of this?'

He snapped it up onto the screen and she nodded. 'Yes. The pelvis has a slight fracture across the acetabulum, here—' she pointed out the fine line across the socket of the hip joint '—and the whole joint has probably destabilised a little in the collision.'

'Collision?'

'Oh, yes, I think so—hasn't the patient been involved in a car accident? Looks like a telescoped front end, with the bulkhead pushing up against the knees and transmitting the force of the impact through into the thighs and pelvis. I expect she was on the left side of the car and the pelvic fracture resulted from her being slammed against the door or the door slammed against her by another vehicle, perhaps? Were there any other injuries?'

'Such as?'

She shrugged. 'Foot or lower leg? Facial? Whiplash to the neck and upper spine? Ribs, maybe, if she was the driver, but I don't think she was.'

'She?'

'Yes, it's a woman,' Frankie said confidently. 'You

can tell from the pelvis—and the name on the X-ray plate!'

His mouth twitched and she felt a ripple of relief. At least he appeared to have a sense of humour in there somewhere!

He nodded thoughtfully and answered her previous question. 'Yes, there were some minor facial and cervical spinal injuries and bruising from the seat belt. The other leg was all right. She was a passenger, travelling on the left of the car in a front right quarter impact. The car then slewed round and hit a wall. The driver was killed outright; so was the rear-seat passenger behind him who wasn't wearing a seat belt. She was lucky to get away with it so lightly.

'So,' he said, leaning back against the desk and bracing his hands on the edge at each side, 'how would you deal with her?'

Frankie chewed her lip slightly. 'I'd fix the femur internally, both because it's a spiral fracture and unstable with traction alone and because the neck of the femur looks stable and I wouldn't want to go and tug on it. At the moment it isn't displaced so I'd want to manage it conservatively if possible and just watch it.

'Also I'd put the other leg in traction to relieve pressure on that acetabulum and rest the damaged tissues in the hip joint.'

'Just like that.'

'If the skin's intact or in good enough condition for the operation and if the soft tissues aren't too badly damaged. I can't tell that, of course, from the X-rays.'

'No. Right, well, she's our first customer.'

'And?'

He raised an eyebrow. 'And what?'

'Was I right with the treatment?'

A grudging smile touched his eyes. 'Yes, you were.'

She had to stop herself forcibly from heaving a sigh

of relief. Instead she turned to the pile of X-ray envelopes on the desk. 'What's next?'

He took down the woman's X-rays and put them away, then snapped another set up onto the screen. 'This man.'

He sat back on the edge of the desk again, and Frankie could feel his eyes boring into her. 'Um—he's got lower leg fractures—ah—is that an old one?'

She swivelled round to look at him and he shrugged nonchalantly. 'You tell me—you're the diagnostician.'

She stifled her retort, turned back to the plates and nodded, running her fingertip down the shin bone and the finer bone—the fibula—beside it. 'Yes—there's an old non-union of the tibia, a mal-union of the fibula and another fracture of the tibia and fibula higher up, a new one this time. Looks like a fracture from a direct blow, and as one end of the tib's free it's probably caused havoc in the soft tissue.'

' "Havoc" is putting it mildly,' he told her, shrugging away from the desk and coming to stand behind her. 'He was a pedestrian. He was hit by a car bumper at this point—' His arm reached round her and as he carried on describing the result of the impact his finger pointed out the area of soft tissue damage, invisible on the X-ray.

It would have been invisible to Frankie anyway, because she was suddenly, chokingly aware of him, of the enticing smell of his skin lurking under the smell of antiseptic, the warmth of his arm against her shoulder, the lean, sinuous forearm dusted with dark curls so very, very close to her face. . .

He muttered something under his breath and moved away, and she released the block of air trapped in her lungs, letting it out on a long, silent sigh, and focused on the X-ray again.

'So what are you intending to do with him?' she

asked in what she hoped was a normal voice.

'Open up the leg at the sight of the old fracture, repair the soft tissue damage and realign the old break, pack it with slivers of bone and put an external fixator on to hold the whole thing. I can't fix it internally because of the risk of infection with the soft tissue injuries, so we'll put screws into all the various fragments, pull them out into line with a little judicious twiddling, and fasten the whole lot onto a rod outside his leg and let it get on with it.

'Hopefully the old one'll heal this time, and the new one's got two chances. I'm not so worried about the fibula; I want to sort the tibia out once and for all.'

He flicked off the light, returned the plates to the envelope and gestured towards the door. 'Shall we go? They're all prepped up and ready for us.'

Watching him operate was a joy. He was careful, precise and meticulous, and Frankie realised with a surge of humility how much she had to learn. Oh, she knew the theory—she'd studied it endlessly—but it was nothing compared to watching the real thing.

And he made it look so easy! Fixing the femur with an intramedullary nail driven down inside the bone had always sounded fairly brutal. In his hands it became a skilled procedure, using imaging techniques to see the nail slowly descending through the femur until it reached the fracture, then the ends aligned so that the nail continued on down the second section.

Finally they were fixed in place with screws through the bone into the nail, and so the bone was held, unable to rotate or slip, with the ends in perfect alignment, and all without disturbing the break in the neck of the femur.

He checked on the image intensifier to ensure that all was as he wanted it, then closed the wound on the thigh and at the top of the femur and straightened up with a sigh.

'Thank you, everyone,' he murmured, and turned to Frankie, peeling off his gloves and dropping the mask down off his face. 'How about a cup of coffee while they prepare the operating room for the next onslaught?'

'Sounds good.'

She followed him out, accepted the cup and listened as he talked to the anaesthetist, Peter Graham. From the conversation she gathered that this was far from the first operation they had performed in the last few hours, and there were at least two more ahead—the man with the fractured lower leg and another new admission from A and E.

Robert Ryder turned to her. 'I don't suppose you'd like to pop down there and have a look at the plates, would you, and report back? Perhaps bring the plates back here and we can study them together.'

'Sure.' She put down her untouched coffee and stood up. 'Um—where is A and E?'

Peter grinned. 'Out the door, turn left, down the corridor to the end and turn left again. You can't miss it.'

She followed his directions and found herself in the busy bustle of a typical accident and emergency department. She found the desk in the middle, collared a staff nurse and introduced herself.

'Oh, you've come about the cyclist. He's in here—it's a nasty mess.'

She opened the curtain to reveal a young man on a trolley, the cot sides up and a drip running in. He was lying motionless, his face pale and clammy, and he looked very shocked.

The staff nurse eased off the thick gauze pad covering the wound on the outside of his left foot, and

Frankie's mouth tightened slightly. It was very badly mangled, bent in at an unnatural angle and with extensive soft tissue injuries. There was a great deal of grit and tarmac ground into the exposed bones, and she winced.

'Not nice, is it?' the staff nurse agreed. 'His X-rays are here.'

Frankie studied them thoughtfully. The bones were nearly all intact, amazingly, but one or two were broken through the ends and would need fixing. The main damage, she could see, was to the soft tissues.

'Do you know what happened?' she asked the nurse.

'He was knocked off his bike and dragged along the ground for a few yards by a car. Luckily for him he had a helmet and leather jacket and gloves on, or he'd be a lot worse off. His little finger's broken as well, by the way—just a minor fracture. We've put a garter strapping on to support it. We've done chest X-rays but there didn't seem to be anything on them. He's complaining of pain in the left shoulder, though.'

'May I see?' she asked, and, studying the plate, she ran her finger lightly along the left collar-bone to the outer end. 'The clavicle's partially dislocated,' she said quietly. 'Must have happened as he landed on that shoulder. We'll have to support that for a while as well. OK, thanks—can I take the plates up to Theatre to show Mr Ryder?'

'Sure. What do you want to do with the patient?'

She turned back to the foot and studied it again. The soft tissue injuries were nasty, infection was likely and the toes were looking discoloured. 'I'm inclined to think he'll want this one next. Is the consent form signed?'

'Yes—his wife's here. Do you want to talk to her?'

She shook her head. 'Not until I've spoken to Mr Ryder. I think I'll ring him and ask him to come down.'

She contacted him on the phone, explained the situation and then had to defend her suggestion that he go in next.

'The soft tissues look awful. I think the circulation could be compromised,' she told him.

'The other man's soft tissues look awful.'

'Is the circulation affected?'

She heard him sigh. 'Apparently not. So you want me to come down?'

'I think you should.'

The phone clicked and she replaced it thoughtfully. Was he cross with her? Perhaps she should have just tacked the man on the end of the list, but she wasn't even officially working and the last thing she wanted to do was blow her chances at this job by fouling up in the first few hours!

She needn't have worried. He came down, took one look at the foot and nodded.

'Let's do him next,' he agreed, and Frankie's fragile ego heaved an enormous sigh of relief. The relief quickly turned to horror, however, when he told her that if she liked jigsaws so much she could do this one.

'Me?' she squeaked.

He rolled his eyes above the mask. 'Sure, you. Why not? Don't worry, I'll tell you blow by blow what I want you to do.'

And so she did her first orthopaedic jigsaw, carefully reinstating the circulation by reconnecting the damaged blood vessels as well as possible. When the foot turned pink again she could have wept with delight.

Ryder, however, kept her feet firmly on the ground and her optimism in the dirt—literally.

'Right,' he said, 'now you can set about picking all those bits of tarmac out of the bone-ends and cleaning up the field before closing the skin.'

It took ages, with both of them working although

the area was quite small, and finally it was cleaned up to his satisfaction.

'Right, we need to screw back that small chip of bone with its ligament attached and we're done,' he told her. 'We won't close it because of the danger of infection. It was a very dirty wound.'

It was indeed, and once the healing was under way it would need skin grafts to cover the area. In the meantime it would be covered with a non-adherent dressing.

Finally he declared the operation finished, and Frankie sagged against the wall outside and looked at the clock in disbelief. It had taken nearly two hours, but she was very pleased with herself—until her boss pointed out that it could and should have been done in half the time.

'Still,' he added with a slight smile that softened his weary eyes, 'you did a good job. Well done.'

High praise. She could have hugged him, but thought better of it and concentrated instead on pouring them another cup of coffee and this time drinking hers quickly before the phone could ring again.

They were lucky. His bleeper didn't squawk until later, when they were back on the ward following up the post-ops, all of whom were doing well.

Mary O'Brien, the ward sister, handed him the phone and he spoke to the switchboard briefly before being connected.

Frankie wasn't really listening, but it was impossible not to hear what he was saying, and anyway she was fascinated.

'What do you mean you're at the station? Jane, you can't do this to me! I'm at work—yes, I know it's a bank holiday. It just means that we're even busier—no, I didn't get the day off; my senior registrar did. He worked Christmas, remember?

'You'll have to get a taxi to the house—what do you mean you haven't got any money? Get a taxi here, then. What about your train fare? Oh, Jane, for heaven's sake!'

He looked at Frankie doubtfully. 'Can you hold the fort? Just for half an hour? My daughter's got herself in a mess.'

'Of course,' Frankie assured him, far from confident. She didn't know the hospital, she didn't know all she felt she should about orthopaedics, even though she'd spent the past month reading solidly on the subject, and she felt totally at sea. In, as they said, at the deep end.

'Mary, look after her for me,' he said to the kindly ward sister, and then, with a wry smile and a weary shake of his head, he strode quickly off the ward and away to his errant daughter.

At least, Frankie assumed she was errant. It certainly sounded as if she was, at least a little.

'Can't his wife drive?' she found herself asking.

Mary O'Brien snorted. 'Oh, yes—but she's in London and it's her the child's run away from yet again. They're divorced—have been for years.'

Frankie blinked, part of her mind registering with interest the fact that his wife no longer lived with him. Then her mind belatedly latched onto the information about the child. 'Run away?' she queried.

'I expect so. I should think there was a wild party last night and she hates it. Nice kid. I expect you'll meet her in a while; he often has to bring her in when she does something like this, poor little scrap.'

Poor little scrap? 'How old is she?' Frankie ventured, suddenly concerned for a little girl torn in the war between irresponsible adults.

'Oh, thirteen or so. Twelve, perhaps?'

So, not a little girl at all but quite a big girl—which

meant either that Robert Ryder was wearing better than he had any right to or that he had started a family somewhat younger than was prudent.

Remembering the warmth of his body and the intoxicating scent of his skin as they'd stood side by side for hours in the theatre, she thought the latter most likely.

As sure as eggs is eggs, she thought, he wasn't any less attractive in his early twenties. It would have taken a very level-headed girl to turn him away if he had switched on the charm. Heavens, even when scowling the man is absurdly attractive!

The door opened and a staff nurse popped her head round the door. 'Mrs Jenkins is in pain—any chance of a boost to her painkillers?'

Mary O'Brien turned to Frankie. 'Would you?'

'Of course.' She stood up and followed the staff nurse out, and was joined a moment later by Mary O'Brien with the keys to the drugs trolley.

'What would Mr Ryder normally give her?' Frankie asked the ward sister.

'Oh, just some stronger tablets—a paracetamol and codeine combination, usually. What did she have yesterday?' They checked the drug chart and then Frankie filled it in and Mary dished out the pills and gave them to the patient.

'Soon have you feeling more the thing,' she said kindly, plumping up the pillows and settling the patient more comfortably against them. She had had osteo-arthritis for years and had been given her second hip replacement three days before, Mary told her. She had refused any opiates and so it was proving difficult to get her pain under control, but she was being very brave about it and the situation was gradually improving.

'She gets tired by the end of the day, though, and in the middle of the night she suffers from it. If we could give her pethidine it would be better, but it makes her terribly sick and she says she'd rather be in pain than be sick.'

'Can't the anaesthetist do something to make her pain-free without nausea?'

Mary smiled. 'I'm sure, but she won't let him try. She's got a bee in her bonnet since she had the other hip done ten years ago, and she can't believe things have moved on that far. She's convinced she's better off like this, and so the poor old dear will just have to suffer for it. It won't be for long. She says bad as it is it's better than her old hip was, so all in all she's quite happy most of the day!'

They went back into the ward office, Mary to do some paperwork, Frankie to scan the notes and try and bone up, so to speak, on some of the cases.

They were sitting quietly working when the door burst open and a tall, slender girl with long, straggly fair hair flounced into the room.

'I suppose I've got to sit here and wait till you've finished—I said I'd be all right at the house!' she grumbled.

Her father followed her, his scowl firmly in place, lines of strain etched round his mouth and eyes.

'Jane, for God's sake, just for once in your life do as you're told, could you? Unlike your mother I have a job to do and responsibilities—'

'Yeah, like me.'

He sighed and stabbed his hands through his hair. 'Yes, like you, and the countless patients out there waiting for a little piece of me, and all the others for whom fate has a little treat in store tonight—I'm afraid, like it or not, you'll have to share me, and for now that means sitting there while I ring Mrs Bailey and see if she can come and look after you this evening—'

'I hate Mrs Bailey!' the girl wailed. 'I don't need a babysitter—I'm thirteen, for heaven's sake! You always baby me—'

'Well, you should have thought of that before you got on the train, shouldn't you?' he said irritably as he punched numbers into the hapless phone.

'Why is it always my fault?' she said unhappily, and Frankie, watching out of the corner of her eye, noticed a gleam of moisture on her lashes. Her father, drumming his fingers on the desk, either didn't see or wasn't impressed. His mouth tightened into an even grimmer, tighter line than before.

'You tell me— Ah, yes, Mrs Bailey. It's Robert Ryder—I wonder if you could do me a favour and keep an eye on Jane for me? No, it was quite unexpected—yes, I know it's a bank holiday— Oh, I'm sorry.' He sighed and ran his hand wearily over his face. 'Forget it. I'm sorry to disturb you. Have a good evening with the family. I'll see you tomorrow.'

He cradled the phone in his hand and turned back to Jane.

'She's got her family for the day. Look, I've just got one or two people I'd like to see, then if Frankie wouldn't mind I could take you home and sort things out.'

He turned to Frankie, a weary entreaty in his eyes. 'Will that be all right?'

She smiled faintly. 'I did say I wouldn't let you down,' she reminded him. 'If you take your bleeper so I can get you in a real emergency I'm sure I can cope.'

He smiled, a tired, grateful smile that didn't quite reach those weary eyes, and left the room.

'So, young lady,' Mary said quietly, 'what's it all about this time?'

'Oh, Mum's latest boyfriend—he and his chums were all sitting about the place doing drugs. It makes

me feel sick to see them all giggling and talking rubbish. It's just such a waste of time.'

She rolled her eyes, and Frankie quickly stifled a
smile. It was no laughing matter, but the girl seemed
at least to have the issue of drug-taking in perspective.

Frankie supposed Jane's father should be grateful
for small mercies. . .

CHAPTER TWO

THE rest of that afternoon and evening was relatively quiet. The A and E staff called Frankie once about an elderly lady who had had a fall and broken her hip, and it was decided to admit her for surgery the following day.

After that there seemed to be nothing to do, so armed with her bleeper Frankie made her way back to the doctors' residence and to the room that for now, at least, was home.

She hadn't unpacked properly the night before, so now she opened her suitcases and put the things away in the drawers, hung up her few dresses and put the cases under the bed. Her books she set out on the shelf above the scarred and battered table, and she was done.

Standing back, she surveyed the room critically and sighed. There wasn't much to show for twenty-eight years, she thought with a touch of melancholy, and then banished it ruthlessly. Pictures were what she needed, she decided—pictures and perhaps some flowers to brighten up the dismal little cell. Maybe a pot plant.

She went and made herself a cup of tea in the communal kitchen, added a kettle to the list of necessities and curled up against her pillows with a book.

She couldn't concentrate. All she could see was her new boss's weary eyes, and osteomyelitis simply couldn't handle the competition.

She put the book down.

So, he was divorced—and living alone, if he'd had

to ring someone to look after his daughter. What a waste, she thought, and then chastised herself for making assumptions. Maybe he liked being alone?

And pigs flew. Nobody liked being alone. Sometimes it was better than an existing bad relationship, but given the choice she imagined most people would choose a good relationship over none at all.

Given the choice. Sometimes, of course, one *wasn't* given the choice. She wouldn't be alone by choice, but fate had played dirty tricks on her and she had ended up alone, in this dismal little room—

She snorted in disgust. The room was temporary, just until she had convinced Mr Ryder that it would be a good idea to take her on permanently. Then she'd get herself a nice little flat and start acquiring some little bits and pieces.

If Mr Ryder took her on.

She shook her head. 'Mr Ryder' was so formal. She wondered if he would expect her to call him that, or if 'sir' would do. . .!

Robert.

She tried the name, and decided it suited him. Solid, dependable, utterly trustworthy. No frills or flounces, just a good, honest name that could have been made for him.

She wondered if he resented the responsibilities that had been thrust on him, and decided that even if he did he would never admit it, not even to himself.

Her brother had resented the responsibility of his younger sister. He loved her, but providing her with a home for the past ten years had taken its toll of their relationship. And now his wife was on the scene. . .

With a sigh she picked up her book again and tried to read, but her eyelids were drooping. She took off her skirt, slipped under the quilt and settled down for a rest. She wouldn't sleep for long. Inevitably her bleeper would squawk and she would have to get up again.

Her breathing slowed, her body quickly adapting to rest. After years of practice it had learned to snatch sleep when it was offered, and cat-napping was a gift she treasured. Within seconds, she was asleep.

Robeert knuckled the sleep from his eyes with one hand, the other clutching the receiver as he struggled to cast aside the dream. 'Have you called Dr Bradley?' Hell, even saying her name made it worse—

'Yes, she's with the patient now. She asked if I could contact you and get you to come in. I'm sorry.'

Robert sighed. 'I'll be right over,' he promised, and throwing the bedclothes off he pulled on his clothes and went into his daughter's room.

'Are you going out?' she mumbled.

'Yes—sorry. Will you be all right?'

'Mmm.'

He dropped a kiss on her cheek, ran downstairs and picked up his jacket and keys on the way out of the door. As he drove the short distance to the hospital, he ran the case through his mind again.

It was the man with the damaged lower leg, the one with the old unhealed fracture who had been hit sideways by a car the night before. They had operated just before lunch and put a fixator on the tibia to support the fractures externally, but the leg had swollen and was now apparently showing symptoms of compartment syndrome, where the sheath surrounding each of the muscles refused to allow sufficient swelling and so caused severe constriction to the muscles and underlying tissues, with resulting serious consequences if they were not rapidly decompressed.

He would require a minor operation called a fasciotomy, literally a slit cut in each of the muscle sheaths to allow for the swelling—assuming that Frankie had got it right.

Dr Bradley. He must remember to call her that. The temptation to call her Frankie was mixed up with all sorts of other forbidden temptations that he didn't even dare consider except in his dreams—and they, he thought disgustedly, should be censored.

He turned into the hospital car park, pulled up in his usual space and headed for the ward. She was there, in the office with the night sister, her head thrown back and a delicious, deep chuckle bubbling up from her throat.

She turned to him with a smile and said, 'Hi,' in her warm honey voice, and his pulse rate soared as the dream came screaming back full force. Damn.

He ignored his body, tugged on his white coat from behind the door and rammed his hands deep into the pockets.

'So, what's the situation?' he asked gruffly.

'Mr Lee's leg. It's started to swell more, and he's now got a tense calf with loss of extension and diminished sensation in the foot.'

'Damn. What have you done?'

'Elevated it, ice-packed the muscles and alerted Theatre. He's had a premed and he's ready when you are.'

'You're confident of the diagnosis?'

One eyebrow arched delicately, and she stood up and gestured to the door. 'He's your patient—I'd be delighted for you to check.'

He grunted and followed her to the patient's bedside. Mr Lee was lying with his leg raised in a 'gutter', packed round with soft wadding to support it off the calf, and Robert could see the tension on the skin. The patient was restless, clearly in pain and the foot was looking discoloured. The calf was certainly swollen all round, and there was no question about the diagnosis.

He swore, softly and comprehensively, and then met Frankie's eyes.

'Well done, Dr Bradley,' he murmured. 'Ever done a fasciotomy?'

She shook her head, the soft, fine hair swinging round her face. 'Not yet,' she said, and the faintest smile touched her eyes.

It was the middle of the night, he was exhausted, and yet still she made him want to smile back. He felt his eyes crinkle. 'Well, as the saying goes, there's no time like the present. You didn't really want to go back to that cold, lumpy bed, did you?'

This time she really smiled. 'Actually I was getting used to it,' she said ruefully.

'Tough,' he growled, but he was unable to stop the quirk of his lips, and she smiled again.

'Come on, then, let's go and do this fasciotomy.'

She was a willing pupil, he had to admit. What his grandfather would have called 'a quick study'. She did only what she was told to do, exactly as she was told to do it, and with skill and sensitivity, as if the scalpel were simply an extension of her fingers. Immediately she released the affected compartments the muscle bulged through the space, colour and warmth returned to the foot and the situation improved.

'Excellent,' he murmured. 'Right, he can go back down as soon as he's recovered from the anaesthetic. I'll be in the hospital for a while—I want to see him after he's come round and make sure we've done enough.'

He stripped off his gloves and gown, dropped them in the bin and turned to Frankie. 'You did a really good job. Well done.'

Wonders would never cease. The man who hadn't wanted to give her the job dishing out such high praise? Frankie was faintly dumbstruck. She peeled off her gloves and gown, dropped them in the bin on top of his and marvelled at her beginner's luck.

'Thank you,' she murmured. 'It wasn't really difficult.'

'No, but it's still possible to make a mess of it.'

She forced herself to meet his eyes. 'I said I wouldn't let you down.'

He smiled, a slow, lazy smile that made her heart thump a little harder. 'So you did. Coffee?'

'Tea?'

'Whatever. Shall we go to the canteen? They usually have various things to eat and I'm starving.'

'I've got a fruit cake,' she said rashly.

'Home-made?'

She should have denied it, but his eyes were so hopeful, as if it had been years—possibly forever— since anyone had made him a cake.

'Yes, home-made,' she said gently. 'It was my Christmas cake, but it never got iced. There didn't seem to be a lot of point—I was on duty so much coming up to Christmas that I didn't have time to ice it, and I was too busy over Christmas to eat it, so it didn't really matter. It was a bit ambitious bothering to make it anyway, I suppose.'

He eyed her curiously. 'Didn't you go home for Christmas?'

She thought of Jeff and his new bride, wrapped up in each other to the exclusion of everyone and everything else. She certainly hadn't been wanted.

Her smile probably didn't reach her eyes, but she tried. 'I don't have a family home any more.'

'I'm sorry.' He sounded contrite, as if he regretted hurting her, and suddenly she wanted to comfort him, to explain that it was all right, it didn't matter any more, it couldn't hurt her now.

It was too soon, though. She didn't know him. Maybe later, after a few weeks or months—if she was still here. . .

'So, do you want to risk it?'

His eyes searched her face and he grinned fleetingly. 'What do you think?'

She laughed. 'Come on, then, or we'll be having it for breakfast.'

They walked in silence through the hospital corridors to her room, and she opened the door with a flourish. '*Voilà*! Welcome to my humble abode.'

He went through the door and peered around. 'God, it is, isn't it? I'd forgotten what hospital rooms are like.'

She laughed and closed the door quietly. 'Aren't you the lucky one? Make yourself at home; I'll get the drinks. Tea or coffee?'

'Oh—coffee, please.' He was thumbing through the textbook she had been unable to concentrate on, and she slipped past him, made the drinks and returned to find him sitting on the end of the bed, one leg hitched up and the book lying open on his lap, asleep.

'I found it riveting too.'

He opened one eye and peered at her, then a slow smile tilted his mouth. 'Sorry. It's been a rather hectic weekend.' He snapped the book shut and sat up, taking the coffee from her. 'So, where's this fabled cake?'

She rummaged under the bed and came out with a cake tin, worried now that it would taste awful and disappoint him.

'I hope you're not expecting Fortnum & Mason's standard,' she joked, stabbing a knife into the centre of the untouched cake and chopping out a wedge.

He winced. 'I'm glad I've already seen you operate, otherwise that would really have worried me!'

She chuckled and handed him the crumbling slice. 'Sorry there aren't any plates—here, have the lid.'

He took the lid and sniffed the cake. 'It smells wonderful.'

'Brandy. Go on, then, try it.'

'What about you?'

She raised an eyebrow. 'I want to see if you die first.'

He grinned and took a bite, then shut his eyes and groaned, keeling slowly over onto the bed.

'Ha ha.'

He opened one eye and mumbled something totally unintelligible, swallowed and tried again. 'I said it's worth dying for.'

Quite unexpectedly she felt her cheeks heat. It was one thing to be complimented for her work, and quite another when his remarks were personal—and somehow the fact that she had made the cake and he was impressed was very personal, almost intimate.

She was disgusted at how pleased she was, and yet she couldn't hold down the happiness. It was absurd that it should matter so much, she thought, and hacked off another wedge for herself.

He was right, though—it was good, even if she said so herself. She finished her chunk, licked her fingers and looked up to find him watching her, a strange expression on his face.

Her breath lodged in her throat and she coughed slightly, looking away from those piercing blue-grey eyes. 'More?' she said, and her voice wavered, to her disgust.

'Um—no, thanks. I thought I'd just go back to the ward and check on Mr Lee, then I ought to go back to Jane.'

He stood up, suddenly big in the tiny room, and she put down her cup and stood too. 'Thanks for coming in.'

He laughed without humour. 'I should be thanking you for covering for me so I could sort Jane out, not the other way round. Oh, well, I'll see you in the morning. Thanks for the coffee and the cake—you can save me a slice for another time.'

He was right beside her now, just inches away, and he paused and lifted a hand.

'You've got a crumb on your lip,' he murmured, and she felt his fingertip like a butterfly's wing against her mouth, easing away the crumb. It lingered, just a heartbeat longer than was necessary, and suddenly the butterfly's wing burned against her skin.

Fire shot through her, and as their eyes locked for a long, aching moment she wondered if he was going to kiss her. Then his hand dropped, and with a muffled sigh he opened the door and was gone.

Robert wasn't enjoying this telephone call, but it had to be made. However, he didn't even try to keep the hard edge out of his voice. 'I thought I made it perfectly clear that during the school holidays you wouldn't entertain your lovers.'

'Oh, Robert, for God's sake, it was New Year's Eve! Everybody entertains!'

'I didn't,' he growled. 'I was at work, earning your maintenance.'

'Jane's maintenance,' his ex-wife reminded him with a bitter cut to her voice. 'If you remember you declined to support me.'

Robert sighed. Not this again. He refused to get drawn in. 'She tells me they were "doing drugs".'

'What a revolting expression, darling! Just a little smoke—'

'I don't care how you phrase it, Jackie, I am not having my daughter exposed to drugs and debauchery!'

There was a mock sigh from the other end. 'Here

we go—trotting out the moral outrage. Just because you don't know how to enjoy yourself any more—'

'I don't consider getting drunk and smoking cannabis with a lover in front of my daughter enjoying myself, and I'm appalled that you should. I'm sorry, Jackie, but you've gone too far this time. Jane's living with me now, for good. I'll contact my solicitor and sort out visitation rights, but she's slept the night in your home for the last time.'

He could feel the tension coming off her. 'Robert, darling, you're overreacting! I promise it won't happen again—'

'No, it won't. I'll arrange to collect all her things this weekend—'

'But Robert, please, think about it! You can't just do this—'

'I can and I am. You've had plenty of chances, Jackie.'

'But the maintenance. . .'

His hand tightened on the receiver and the plastic creaked ominously. 'To hell with the maintenance. As you've just pointed out, it wasn't for you anyway, but don't worry, I'll make sure you don't suffer.'

He cradled the poor unfortunate receiver with more force than was necessary and flexed his fingers absently. He must be mad. How was he going to look after Jane? She had no friends in the area, and he was working all day and often at the weekends.

Had he been hasty?

He rammed his fingers through his hair and swore, softly and comprehensively. Would it never end?

He heard a sound behind him and turned his head slowly to see his daughter, clad in her nightshirt, leaning against the doorpost and eyeing him warily as he sprawled in the big old chair.

'Mum?' she asked.

'Yes. I've just told her you're living with me now.'

Jane hovered, chewing her lip unhappily. 'Are you sure you want me?' she asked tentatively. 'I make your life so complicated.'

He couldn't deny it. His life had been complicated by her presence ever since she had been conceived fourteen years before, when he was just a green medical student with more hormones than sense, but want her? Oh, yes. . .

He held out his arms. 'Come here, sweetheart.'

She watched him for a second, then shrugged away from the doorpost and crossed to him, curling up on his lap the way she had as a little girl, her head nestled on his shoulder, her fragrant hair tickling his nose, her light frame angular now and leggy like a foal's.

He snuggled her deeper into his arms, rested his chin against her head and sighed. 'Love you, JJ.'

'Love you too, Dad,' she mumbled, and he felt her slim arms creep round his chest and squeeze.

Anger rose in him, anger at his ex-wife for so callously and selfishly following her own path to the detriment of Jane's happiness, anger too at her money-grubbing plea about the maintenance.

'Don't be angry with her, Dad. She can't help it. It's just the way she is.'

He sighed and stroked the sweetly scented hair. 'It just makes me angry when she hurts you.'

Jane sat up on his lap and shook her head. 'She doesn't hurt me.'

'She disappoints you.'

Jane nodded. 'Yeah.'

'I'm sorry.'

'For what? Not choosing my mother more carefully?' She ruffled his hair affectionately. 'Don't be silly. Are you going to work?'

'I have to. I've got a new registrar and she got flung

in a bit at the deep end yesterday.'

'Mmm. Frankie. I like her; she's got nice eyes.'

His mouth quirked in a fleeting smile. 'Yes—yes, she has. She's probably got bags under them by now. I'd better go and give her the day off, I think.'

He patted Jane's shoulder, and she slid off his lap and stretched, her nightshirt rising up to show endless skinny legs. She's grown even more, he realised with a start, and she's turning into a woman. Dear God, can I cope?

He stood up and hugged her briefly, dropped a kiss on her soft hair and let her go. 'Will you be all right?'

She rolled her eyes. 'Dad, for God's sake! I got here from London all right.'

'Yes, well, we won't talk about that. There's food in the fridge and Mrs Bailey will be in later to clean up a bit and cook supper for us.'

'I could do that.'

He chuckled. 'Jane, when you were last here a week ago you couldn't even make your own bed. I think we'll let Mrs Bailey do it—maybe she'll teach you how to cook if you ask her nicely.'

Jane rolled her eyes again. 'Dad, I know how to cook. What do you think Mum eats in the holidays when her boyfriends aren't allowed to take her out for dinner?'

He smiled, but inwardly he seethed again that she should be so cynical so young. Damn Jackie. When he caught up with her he'd have a few choice words to say, and out of JJ's earshot, too, so he didn't have to pull his punches.

'I'll ring you later.'

'Daddy, I'll be fine.'

He grinned at her. 'OK, love. Take care.'

'You too.' She reached up on tiptoe and kissed his

cheek. 'Have a good day. Say thank you to Frankie for me for covering for you.'

Frankie was shattered.

It was easy enough to keep up the cheerful, determined 'I can do it' front while Robert was around. When she was on her own, however, doubts began to assail her.

His praise on her first day had helped enormously, but all the time she was working she was desperately conscious of being under scrutiny. Not that that mattered. She didn't worry about being watched—it was a valuable safety net for the patients during her learning process—but she was beginning to wish she hadn't made the suggestion about being on trial.

After less than a week she was finding the process unbelievably tiring, and every time he moved out of sight her cheery smile slipped.

Apparently it didn't go unnoticed. She was sitting in the staff coffee-lounge one lunchtime after a gruelling clinic that had had all the subtlety of a finals viva, sipping strong coffee and chewing methodically but without enthusiasm on a Danish pastry, when a shadow fell across her lap.

'Mind if I join you?'

She looked up to find a man of about her own age, dressed in theatre pyjamas, his dark hair rumpled and untidy, a cautious half-smile on his generous mouth.

'Do,' she answered. He looked friendly and approachable and not about to pounce, she thought with relief. She was too damn tired and strung out to deal with Tarzan today.

'You're new, aren't you?' he asked, settling himself down with his anti-static boots propped on the table and the coffee-cup balanced on his lap.

'Yes. I've been here since Monday.'

His grey eyes assessed her thoughtfully and the cautious smile touched his lips again. 'Were you tired when you arrived, or has this place got to you already?'

She laughed. 'A bit of each. I did a silly thing. I talked myself into a job on a trial basis, and now I feel I can't breathe spontaneously without it being noted down.'

He chuckled. 'You're Robert Ryder's junior reg, aren't you? I gather he's excellent.'

'Yes, he is. Rather too excellent. The shortfall is all the more obvious,' she said with wry self-mockery.

The young doctor laughed softly and leant forward, his hand outstretched. 'I'm Gavin Jones—Oliver Henderson's junior reg.'

She shook the firm, dry hand. 'Frankie Bradley.'

'Frankie—that's unusual.'

'Frances really,' she said with a little shudder.

Gavin smiled. 'Frances is fine but Frankie suits you better. So—you're on trial. Wow. I remember when I made a foul-up as a houseman and Ross Hamilton came down on me like a ton of bricks. I couldn't breathe after that either without him watching me!'

'What did you do?'

'Took out an appendix on a girl with Munchausen's—but you'll be safe there. It doesn't happen in orthopaedics. Either it's broken or it isn't!'

She chuckled. 'I hope you're right. I'll probably end up recommending arthroscopy on someone's knee when there's nothing at all wrong with it.'

He drained his coffee-cup and put it down on the table. 'Um—I don't suppose you fancy a drink tonight?'

The idea was suddenly immensely appealing. 'That would be lovely,' she told him, a smile softening her tired eyes.

'Seven? I'll pick you up—I take it you're living in?' She nodded wryly. 'Are you?'

'For my sins. I'm only just back here—I've been away for a while as a registrar in Cambridge—and I haven't got a flat sorted out yet. I don't think it'll be long, though. Those rooms are the pits.'

She laughed with him, and watched as he left the room. She was still smiling as her bleeper went, and with a sigh she got up and went over to the phone.

'Dr Bradley,' she told the switchboard.

'Putting you through,' the voice replied, and suddenly there was a young, hesitant girl on the line.

'Um—is that Frankie?'

'Yes, it is. Is that Jane Ryder?'

'Yeah—listen, can you do me a favour? It's my father's birthday today and I'm cooking him a special meal tonight, and I thought it would be nice if you could join us. It'd make it more of a celebration, somehow, and give me a chance to thank you for bailing Dad out so he could fetch me from the station and bring me home. So,' she said, all in a rush and running out of breath, 'will you come?'

She sounded so hopeful, and Frankie didn't have the heart to disappoint her. Besides which, it would be an ideal opportunity to get to know her enigmatic and very reserved boss a little better. She could always put Gavin off for another time.

'Yes, of course I'll come.'

'Are you sure? It's probably the last thing you want to do—'

'Nonsense,' Frankie interrupted. 'I'll look forward to it. What time?'

'Seven-thirty? Oh, and do you like chicken curry?'

'Ah. Um, Jane, I'm vegetarian.'

There was a horrified silence. 'So I guess that means

you don't like chicken,' she said eventually.

'Look, if it messes things up for you I don't need to come, Jane.'

'But I want you to!' the girl wailed.

'Then I will. Don't worry about feeding me—I can have all the accompaniments.'

'Oh. Well, I could do you some veg in a curry sauce—would that do?'

'That would be lovely,' she said firmly. 'Don't worry about me; cook what your father likes. It's his birthday. How do I get there?'

Jane gave her the directions—somewhat haphazard, but hopefully she could unravel them in the dark.

'What's the phone number, in case I get lost?'

Jane rattled off the number, then added, 'By the way, don't tell him—it's a surprise.'

It was raining, just to add insult to injury. Gavin had been understanding—to a point. 'Had a better offer?' he'd ribbed gently.

'I'm sorry,' she'd apologised. 'Perhaps another time?'

His smile had been wry. 'Yeah—maybe. Have a good evening.'

She felt she'd disappointed him, but there was no point in encouraging him if he had any ideas about their relationship. He was a nice man, but he didn't do anything for her—unlike Robert—

'Damn!' She slithered to an undignified halt and reversed back, peering at the road sign. Was this it? No. Damn again. She drove on till she found a pub, then went in and asked the barman the way.

He yelled across the bar, 'Hey, Fred, how d'you get to Ryder's old place? Is that first left or second?'

'Doc Ryder?' Fred shrugged away from the wall by the dartboard, picked his teeth thoughtfully as he sauntered towards them and eyed Frankie with interest. 'Goin' there, are you?'

'If I can find it.'

He nodded. 'Back down to the bottom of the hill, turn right, go about two miles, first left, along about couple hundred yards or so on the right. Thatched place, it is. Old Tudor job—white gates.'

All eyes were on her, as if a woman visiting Robert Ryder was a rare and notable occurrence.

She forced a smile. 'Thank you. I'm sure I'll find it now.' She made for the door, and was just opening it when Fred hailed her.

'Hear his daughter's home.'

She turned back slightly. 'Yes.'

'Good job, too. The mother's not worth her weight in chicken sh—ah, manure.'

Amidst the ribald laughter she made her escape from the pub, running across the potholed car park in the slashing rain.

Just before she reached her car she put her foot into a pothole, jarred her ankle and splashed muddy water all the way up her clean tights. Swearing comprehensively and most satisfyingly under her breath, she slammed the car door, started the engine and drove back down the hill, along a miserable, rutted lane for two miles or more, until she was sure that Fred had got it wrong.

Then suddenly there was a little turning, an even smaller road, and on the right a low, thatched house with lights blazing a welcome from all the windows. There was an old-fashioned lamppost at the entrance, and in its warm glow she saw the name on the opened gate.

Freedom Farm. . .

CHAPTER THREE

IT WAS a lovely evening. Jane had gone to huge lengths to prepare a meal to remember, and Robert was obviously touched and very, very proud.

The fact that Robert clearly hadn't been expecting her was obvious from the look on his face when he opened the door. However, he quickly recovered his poise, accepted the bottle of vintage port with a polite murmur of protest and then showed her through into the drawing room.

It was spotlessly tidy, a lovely, heavily beamed room with formal furniture and an air of expectancy. While Robert fetched her a drink she found herself looking round the room and trying to work out what was wrong with it, because it lacked something indefinable but very, very important.

Warmth? Not heat but warmth—love, perhaps. She sensed that it was a room not often used, a room where shared laughter and tender words never echoed, and so the walls were blank, waiting for history to carve itself into the atmosphere. Or recent history, at least. The aged walls and heavy oak beams were soaked in history, but it seemed suppressed, as if it needed the heat of passion to bring it all to life.

She sensed that Robert, too, was uncomfortable in there, as if there was another room, another place that was his retreat—a place where he would rather be. They had perched in there, sipping sherry and making stilted conversation, until Jane came in and announced that their meal was ready.

She was flushed a dull rose, and her cheek was

adorned with a dollop of curry sauce, but her eyes were full of eager anticipation and dread in equal measure.

How wonderful, Frankie thought achingly, to have someone to try so hard to please you. The look in Jane's eyes reminded Frankie of her brother's wife, eager to please, nothing too much trouble.

And how wonderful, she thought, to have someone you wanted to please, be it father, husband—lover?

Jane ushered them through into the dining room and seated them at the worn and well-loved mahogany table, then served up the meal from the vast number of bowls and dishes that were laid out on its surface.

'JJ, this looks wonderful,' Robert said in astonishment, and the girl flushed with pride and caught her bottom lip between her teeth.

Heavens, what a pretty girl, Frankie thought, and then wondered how Robert would cope without the moderating feminine influence of a wife. Would he allow Jane any freedom to explore her budding womanhood?

She thought not—or not easily. He clearly adored her, and the thought of her turning into a woman with a woman's needs and wants would torture him, Frankie was sure.

The food broke the ice a little. OK, the rice was a little cold, and Frankie had a sneaking suspicion that her 'vegetable' curry was a few frozen veg quickly boiled and then doused in the chicken curry sauce. But she decided that Jane's sensibilities were more important than her own and ate it with every appearance of enjoyment, and gradually the conversation warmed and laughter trickled in.

'So, how are you coping with the old bossy-boots?' Jane asked her at one point with a wicked twinkle at her father. 'Is he awful at work?'

Frankie grinned and studied him. 'Awful? Only five days a week.'

'You haven't worked with him on Saturday and Sunday yet,' Jane pointed out.

'So I haven't. I expect he'll be even worse then, as it's the weekend.'

Robert closed his eyes and gave a mock sigh. 'Maligned, I am. I thought I'd actually been the perfect boss.'

Frankie chuckled. 'Of course. I expect you're really very kind under that grim and forbidding exterior.'

His eyes flew open and he studied her in genuine astonishment. 'Grim and forbidding? Really?'

She relented. 'No, not really. Mostly you're quite civilised. You only bite if I'm particularly stupid or you're particularly hungry.'

It was an unfortunate choice of words. Something flared in his eyes, and Frankie felt the heat scorch her cheeks. She dropped her head forward slightly and her hair swung down and screened her blush. Damn, what was going on? She'd thought she'd imagined the heat between them on her first night, when he'd brushed the crumb from her lip—but perhaps not?

She hadn't lied, in fact. He had been a little grim and forbidding. Maybe this uninvited attraction was the cause? He probably resented it for getting in the way of a professional relationship.

Well, he was safe with her. Her career was more important than her private life—for now, at least.

Finally the meal was finished and Jane ushered them out into the drawing room again where she served them coffee, then curled up beside her father on the settee with a cup of hot chocolate.

'That was wonderful, JJ,' he told her, and the warmth in his eyes and voice made Frankie's throat ache. She busied herself with her coffee, giving them room while they exchanged quiet, gentle words. Did he know how lucky he was? she wondered. Or Jane? Did she have any idea how precious her father's love was, or how fleeting?

She swallowed the lump in her throat and stirred the cream into her coffee, watching the black and white merge to a dull tan.

Like her life. The contrast was gone, leaving only work to bring any colour or meaning to it. She wasn't unhappy, but she wasn't happy either. Content?

She probably should be grateful.

She listened to the soft music playing in the background, and the gentle murmur of Robert's voice mingled with Jane's lighter tones. What was she doing here? Robert didn't want her here, stirring up the undertones and making things difficult. She ought to go—

'Goodnight, Frankie. Thank you for coming.'

She looked up, blinking, thinking herself dismissed, and found instead that Jane was on her feet and hovering at the door. 'I have to go to bed,' she said with a little grimace.

Frankie laughed wryly. 'Don't knock it. It wasn't so long ago I would have given my eye-teeth for someone to send me to bed.'

Jane grinned. 'Yeah, well, we all want what we can't have, don't we? Oh, well, 'night, all.'

''Night, Jane—and thank you for a lovely meal. I really enjoyed it. In fact, talking of bed. . .' She set her cup down with a little rattle. 'I must go—I've been here for hours—'

'Oh, you don't have to go. Stay and have another coffee with Dad—there's tons in the pot. 'Night, Dad.'

'Goodnight, JJ—and thank you, darling. It was a wonderful birthday treat.'

She grinned, her apprehension gone, and flitted

through the door. Seconds later she reappeared, a rather more sheepish look on her gamine face.

'Um—don't worry about the kitchen, by the way, Dad. I'll fix it tomorrow.'

Robert closed his eyes as she flitted off again, humming. 'Oh, God,' he groaned. 'I have a bad feeling. . .'

Frankie chuckled, her melancholy drifting away on his sigh. 'Come on. She's done enough. I'll help you sort it out before I go.'

She followed him into the kitchen, cannoning into his back in the doorway. The grunt of disbelief echoed through his chest and, peering over his shoulder, she scanned the kitchen.

'Yup—looks like a teenager just cooked a meal,' she said cheerfully. 'I'll wash; you dry up and put away.'

Those few words made it sound so simple. They didn't begin to touch the bottoms of the pans, caked and burnt with rice and custard and curry sauce, or the endless pots and jars and packets strewn across the worktops—and over it all the fine, crunchy scatter of demerara sugar. . .

'My God! I feel as if I've run a marathon! How could she manage to use so many things?'

With a heartfelt sigh Robert threw himself down into a saggy old chair and waved at its counterpart on the other side of the woodburner.

'Make yourself at home,' he told her, his eyes drifting down and a deep, contented groan rumbling from his big chest.

She looked at him, sprawled across the ancient chair, and, kicking off her shoes, she tucked her feet up and eased herself into its partner's arms. It swallowed Frankie whole, snuggling her down into its intimate depths and cosseting her like an old hen with a chick.

'Mmm,' she murmured contentedly.

Robert cranked open an eye and grinned. 'I hate the drawing room,' he grumbled. 'It was JJ's idea to use it. "You've got a guest coming," she told me—I had no idea it was you.'

She smiled awkwardly. 'I'm sorry. I should have warned you this afternoon.'

He waved his hand dismissively. 'No, not at all. She likes surprises—like turning up here on New Year's Day. Surprising me is what she does best. Can I get you a drink—that rather nice port you so wickedly bought me, perhaps?'

She was tempted, but refused. 'No, I'm driving. If you're having one I'll have a sip, but that's all.'

'Coffee?'

'It'll be cold.'

'I can make more.'

She looked at him, slumped wearily in the chair, and shook her head. 'Don't bother. Just sit there and relax.'

'Sure?'

She nodded and he closed his eyes, dropping his head back against the welcoming upholstery and sighing softly under his breath. 'I'll have a port in a minute,' he mumbled.

Frankie watched him for a moment, noting the dark crescents of his lashes—ridiculously long and wasted on a man, she thought with a little smile—and the soft fullness of his mouth, relaxed in rest and suddenly, enticingly kissable—

She caught herself up short. What was she thinking about? This was her boss—the man who wielded power over her future—the only thing between her and a career in orthopaedic surgery. She had no business thinking about kissing his mouth, however lush and warm and inviting it might be. . .

Her eyes dropped, away from the temptation of that mouth, down over the shadowed jaw, strongly carved and firm, decisive, typical of the man; and on, past the small swelling of his Adam's apple, resting in the V of his shirt. The tie he'd been wearing had long gone so that it didn't trail in the washing-up. There was a little tuft of hair, a curl, like the little girl who had one in the middle of her forehead. When he was good, he was very, very good, and when he was bad. . .

A shiver ran over her and her eyes trailed on, down over the broad chest under the scant covering of the fine silk shirt, the dark hair underneath casting shadows where it lay between his nipples and down the centre of his chest, not too much so that he looked like a gorilla, but just enough to emphasise his masculinity—not that it needed emphasising.

His waist was slim and neat, his stomach board-flat and firm. His hips were lean, taut, his legs, crossed at the ankle, long and straight and well muscled, cradling the discreet but very masculine bulge that she refused to let her eyes dwell on. One trouser leg was hitched up a little and she could see the dark dusting of hair on his shin above his sock. She had a crazy urge to touch it, to see if it was tough and wiry or if it felt as soft as it looked. . .

The curl at his neck drew her, too, like a magnet. She wanted to thread her finger into it and wind it round, tugging it gently, knowing it would inflame him.

She let her eyes trail slowly up over his body again, taking in all the subtle details—the steady rise and fall of his chest just visible in the slanting light—and that curl again, tantalising her. The light gleamed on it, shifting as his chest rose and fell.

'Frankie, what the hell are you doing?' he said softly, his voice roughened and gravelly.

Her eyes widened with shock and flew up to meet his. She licked her suddenly dry lips. 'I thought you were asleep.'

He shook his head slightly. 'Just resting after that horrendous kitchen.'

The silence stretched between them, Frankie's heart beating like a little bird trapped in her chest as her eyes locked with his and she saw through the weariness and the responsibility, past the professional man and dedicated father to the raw, aching need beneath.

'Robert?' Her mouth moved on his name but no sound emerged.

A log fell in the fire, hissing softly and breaking the silence. He looked away, shifting in his seat, one long leg crossing over the other knee.

Hiding his response? Dear God, she couldn't hide hers. She wanted to cross the room to him, unfold that leg and sit on his lap, wrap her arms round his neck and lower her lips to his, claiming that beautiful, needy mouth—

'Frankie, for God's sake!'

Her eyes jerked to his again and her breath shuddered in her chest. 'I think I'd better go home,' she muttered and, leaping up, she slid her feet back into her shoes and then opened the door.

A cupboard. Oh, God, where was the way out?

'Frankie?'

His voice, soft and raw, was right behind her. She stood still, her shoulders stiff and ramrod-straight, waiting for him to make the next move.

His hands, warm and gentle, settled over her shoulders and drew her back against his chest. 'Frankie, we can't let this get in the way. We have to work together.'

'I know that,' she mumbled.

'It's just like sheet-lightning—crazy but harmless so long as you don't get too close. It'll go away if we ignore it.'

She nodded, but she could feel the thud of his heart against her back, and lower down the hard jut of his very male response against the base of her spine.

She moved away slightly. 'Where's my coat?' she asked, her voice catching, breaking in the middle like an adolescent boy's.

He opened another door which led back to the hall and retrieved her coat from the arm of an old oak settle. 'Here.' He helped her into it, settling it with elaborate care around her shoulders, his hands sliding down her arms to her wrists, the heat of them burning her.

She slipped her hands away from his and turned to say goodnight.

It was a mistake.

His eyes were like windows on his emotions, and the wild, aching need in them was her undoing. It so exactly matched her own. Without thought, without reason, she moved into his arms and, threading her fingers through his hair, drew his mouth down to hers.

His groan filled her mouth, then his arms eased up to cradle her against his chest as he gave himself up to the kiss. Their tongues met, retreated, sought again and found, and with an agonised sound Robert cupped her head with one hand and deepened the kiss.

Her legs threatened to crumble, and as if he knew he slid one strong, powerful leg between hers to support her.

It just made it worse, the contact of that lean, hard-muscled thigh against the burning need that drove her. A sob rose in her throat, and with a muttered curse Robert lifted his head, moved his thigh away and wrapped her hard against his chest.

'I'm sorry,' he rasped, his breathing jagged and uneven, a counterpoint to her own.

She shook her head, unable to speak, and her hands smoothed over his back, her palms running lightly over the broad columns of muscle bracketing his spine. The silk shirt was damp, his skin hot and enticing.

Her actions weren't soothing, she realised, either to her or to him.

She dropped her hands and moved away. She couldn't meet his eyes, afraid of what she might see, and she would have opened the front door and run away into the night if he hadn't caught her chin and tipped it, forcing her to look at him.

His lips were full, swollen slightly and reddened by their kiss, and a dull flush lay on his cheeks, but it was his eyes that stunned her, hot and filled with frustration but also determined and somehow withdrawn, as if the incident was closed and would remain so.

'Are you all right?' he asked softly.

She nodded. 'I'll live.'

His smile was wry and didn't quite reach his eyes. He opened the door and walked her to her car. 'Goodnight, Frankie. Thank you for your company—and the port.'

'You're welcome.' The social platitude came automatically. Her mind was elsewhere, lingering on that kiss and the dull ache it had left behind.

She opened the door and slid behind the wheel, but before she could close the door he muttered something and bent towards her, one hand on the roof of the car, the other cupping her chin as he feathered her mouth with his lips.

'Sleep tight,' he murmured, and then he straightened, slammed the door and let her go.

Sleep? she thought. Fat chance, Ryder, after that kiss. . .

'One for you, I think.'

'What?' Frankie was horrified. She had spent the whole weekend worrying about how she would manage to work with him after that searing kiss they had shared, and he didn't show any sign of remembering it. On the contrary, he was all brisk professionalism—and hurling her in at the deep end! 'Look, you have to be joking!' she protested. 'I can't do a hip replacement!'

'Of course you can. Nothing to it. I'll be there, Frankie.'

She eyed him doubtfully, trying hard not to notice the little nick on his chin where he had cut himself shaving, and that lock of hair that would escape and fall down, just crying out for her fingers—

'I'm not sure I can cope,' she said more firmly, dragging her wicked, wilful mind back into order. 'If I could just watch you one more time—'

'Frankie, you've watched several,' he pointed out fairly. 'You have to start somewhere.'

'But it's so important.'

'Everything we do is important, from setting a little finger to dealing with a broken neck.'

Frankie had visions of a broken neck—hers, after she failed to measure up to Robert Ryder's exacting standards.

'I seem to remember at your interview you said you wouldn't let me down,' he murmured, sneaking in a low blow that was right on target.

'OK, OK! I'll do it. Just scrub and be there in case I foul up.'

'Are you kidding? I don't intend to let you out of my sight.'

Perversely Frankie wasn't reassured. They scrubbed, gowned up and went into the operating room as the patient was wheeled in. Then, after checking the notes and the X-rays and the marks on the patient's skin— 'Wouldn't do to fix the wrong hip,' Robert joked, sending a shiver down her spine—they were ready to start.

The scrub nurse handed her a scalpel, and she took a steadying breath. Was he going to help, or just give her enough rope to hang herself?

'Where are you going to make the incision?' he asked quietly.

'Here?' She drew a line with the scalpel a fraction above the skin.

'Fine. Go on, then.'

So she did, exposing the layers and systematically working her way down to the joint.

'Right, the replacement we're using is a Charnley, so the first job is to detach the greater trochanter. Where will you do that?'

Again she showed him, pointing out where she would detach the outer projection of the thigh bone with its attached muscles, and again he agreed and watched silently while she did so, then as she struggled to dislocate the head of the femur from the hip joint. Damn, she thought, he was right—it *is* physical!

'There's a knack,' he said helpfully after she had struggled unsuccessfully for some seconds. 'Put the limb so, and just—'

With his hands over hers, using very little pressure, just leverage and persuasion, he popped the hip joint apart.

'Hmm,' she muttered, and could have sworn he smirked under the mask.

'Right, now can you see the damage to the head of the femur and to the cup of the acetabulum? No wonder she's been in pain.'

The cartilage covering the joint was worn and in places completely gone, exposing the delicate and sensitive bone beneath.

'Ouch,' Frankie muttered.

'Ouch indeed. She's going to feel the benefit the moment she comes round, I would think. That must be like walking on a permanent fracture. Right, you need to take off the head of the femur.'

'Here?'

He agreed and watched her again, talking her through the reaming out of the cup in the pelvis and the cementing in of the new socket, the filing of the inside of the femur to accept the long shaft of the new femoral head and its careful and precise insertion with cement to ensure a permanent and stable bond.

'Mmm,' he said as she finished reattaching the point of the thigh bone, the greater trochanter, with its muscles still intact. What did 'Mmm' mean? she wondered. Had she fouled up?

He met her eyes over the patient then looked away. 'Right, close her up, Frankie; we've got two more to do before lunch.'

She sutured with her usual meticulous care, but tried to hurry, conscious of the press of time and the list of patients prepped up and waiting in the wings, as it were. What had she done wrong? Had she wired the trochanter back too tight? Too loose? In the wrong place? Or was it something she'd done earlier—her cementing, perhaps?

As the patient was wheeled out to Recovery and Frankie and Robert left the room her legs felt like jelly.

She stripped off her gloves, dropped her mask and gown into the bin, washed her hands and face and stood facing the mirror, blotting her skin dry with a paper towel and watching him.

'Well?' she said finally, unable to bear the suspense.

He straightened up, water dripping off his chin, and grinned. 'You'll do.'

Her legs almost gave way. 'Rat,' she muttered under her breath, but he must have heard her.

He tutted softly. 'Show a little respect, Dr Bradley.'

She closed her eyes wearily. 'I have great respect

for you, sir,' she said with just the slightest trace of sarcasm.

He chuckled. 'Of course I could have watched you struggle with that dislocation for another ten minutes. You would never have got it out the way you were going about it.'

'As you said,' she told him, turning to face him and dropping the paper towel in the bin, 'it's a knack, and one I can soon learn.'

'Well, hopefully you've learnt it because you'll have to do the next one quicker than that.'

She felt her jaw sag slightly. 'The next?'

'Uh-huh. The next two, actually. You're here to learn, Frankie. You won't do that if I mollycoddle you for ever.'

He didn't, either. Throughout the whole of the next operation he watched in silence, saying nothing, raising an eyebrow if she glanced up to check with him that she was doing it right, until in the end she was driven almost to distraction.

'Help me!' she said finally.

'Why? You're doing fine. I'll tell you when you go wrong.'

Slightly reassured, she continued with the operation, gaining confidence as all seemed to be going to plan. Then, as she was setting the cup into the acetabulum, he intervened.

'You've got the angle of the cup too steep. The joint will dislocate if you leave it like that. Tip it more, like so—' he rearranged it '—and the joint will be more stable.'

'Thank you,' she mumbled, chastened, her new-found confidence ground to dust. The change in angle seemed so slight. . .

'You'll soon get used to judging it,' he assured her, and turned to the anaesthetist. 'I gather Oliver had a crisis over the weekend,' he said, and she listened with half an ear as they discussed the sudden and unexpected death of a patient whom one of the general surgeons had operated on the previous day.

She struggled with the hip prosthesis, reaming out the shaft and offering up the prosthesis until she was happy with the fit, and all the time she thought that Robert was totally absorbed in his conversation and paying her no attention. She could stick the damn thing in upside down and he wouldn't notice—

'Rotate it back a little—that's better. You've reamed it out a little wide. Be sure and pack the cement well into the cavity when you reinsert it. So, do you think there'll be any legal implications?'

Legal implications? she thought in panic, and then realised they weren't talking about her making the space slightly too large, but about the death of the patient at the weekend. Heaving a mental sigh of relief, she cemented in the joint, reattached the trochanter and closed up.

As she finished, she looked up and met the anaesthetist's eye.

'She's all yours,' she said, and he winked and began to reverse the anaesthetic.

Robert glanced casually at the suture line, nodded so slightly that if she hadn't been looking for it she wouldn't have seen it, and headed for the door.

And that was it. No further comment. She almost expected him to take himself off for an early lunch and leave her with the last patient, but he didn't.

'I'll help with this one because we're running a little behind,' was his only remark, and once again she had the joy of watching him work, with a combination of speed and accuracy that she could only hope to imitate.

When they were done—still over time, but not by as much—he tugged off his gloves, chucked his gown and mask and hat into the bin and met her expectant eyes.

'I believe we'll make a surgeon of you yet,' he said calmly.

Her heart leapt at the praise, but she kept her delight out of her voice. 'Even though I'm just a feeble woman?' she challenged.

He snorted rudely. 'Feeble? Who ever gave you that idea?' He glanced at the clock, then back at Frankie. 'Quick shower, lunch and go over where you went wrong and then we've got the clinic. I'll let you do it with my SR—he's back from his holiday today and will probably be exhausted.'

So it hadn't been perfect, then, if there were things to go over.

She was showered and dressed before him, to her great satisfaction and his amazement. They walked briskly down to the staff canteen, and she was glad she was so tall, because without her long legs she would have had to run to keep up with him.

They discussed her failings—at least, Robert listed them and Frankie listened in horrified silence as he seemed to condemn her out of hand, and then he sat back, grinned, and said, 'All in all, it was a good morning's work, really.'

Good? Relief loosened her control on her emotions, and a little bubble of laughter gurgled up in her throat.

He frowned, those dark, forbidding brows crawling together above his icy blue-grey eyes. It was funny, but she didn't find his scowl at all forbidding any more. 'I thought you were getting ready to sack me,' she told him honestly.

'Sack you? If it gets that bad, believe me, I'll banish you from the theatre and take over rather than let you carry on. No, you were fine, just inexperienced. You won't make the same mistakes again; I'm quite confident of that.'

He lounged back in his chair, coffee-cup propped on his belt, and eyed her thoughtfully. 'Jane sends her love,' he said finally. 'She asked me to thank you for coming over on Friday and giving up your evening to eat with us.'

Frankie's face warmed at the memory of that meal, and the kiss that followed it. 'It was my pleasure,' she said honestly. 'It was a lovely meal—please tell her that again. I really enjoyed it.'

'And the clearing-up?'

They chuckled together, and she thought yet again how laughter softened his features and brought warmth to those lonely, hungry eyes.

'Is she settling down now with you?' Frankie asked, concerned for Jane's happiness in the turmoil of her parents' shattered relationship.

'She's gone back to boarding school—she weekly boards in Cambridge. I have to fetch her every Friday evening and take her back every Sunday—and she's got no friends of her own age around us.'

He sighed and ran his hand through his hair. 'I worry about her. It's OK when I'm not on call, but if I am she's left to her own devices and I'm concerned about that. She's at a vulnerable age, and you know the old saying about the devil making work for idle hands.'

'She's a good girl, Robert. She's very together. I don't think you need to worry about her being led astray—and anyway, who by?'

He shrugged. 'I just wish she had a friend, someone to go shopping with, do all the things girls do. I can't go round with her trying on clothes and looking at jewelry.'

'I can.'

His eyes speared her. 'You? Why would you do that?'

She lifted her shoulders slightly. 'Because I'm lonely here too? Because I like to do girly things as well, and I haven't got anyone to do them with? She reminds me so much of myself at the same age, Robert. Believe me, if I take her round town with me it will be as much for me as for her.'

'And you'd do that without being paid?' He sounded almost amazed, as if it was unheard of for anyone to want to do something for him or his daughter without a catch. Then his face changed and he eyed her suspiciously. 'You're not gay?' he said harshly.

She set down her cup with exaggerated care and stood up. 'If you can still think that, after the way I kissed you on Friday night, you need your radar checked,' she said quietly, and walked out of the canteen.

She heard a crash, a muffled curse and then he was beside her, grabbing her arm and dragging her to a halt.

She stopped, pointedly removed his hand from her arm and glared at him. 'You have a warped and damaged mind,' she told him coldly.

He closed his eyes. 'No, I haven't. I've got a daughter I love very much, who's been exposed to more than enough trauma in her young life without me unwittingly exposing her to any more. It's just that after the example of her mother I can't believe any woman would do anything for anyone without a price.'

'Then I feel sorry for you—all of you,' Frankie said gently, and walked away.

CHAPTER FOUR

FRANKIE had the rest of the afternoon to regret her outburst. The SR, David Hunt, was quietly methodical if a rather boring young man, and she worked alongside him with only part of her brain in gear. The rest was locked very definitely in combat with the thorny problem of the advisability of hurling insults at her boss when she was still very much on trial.

Her clinic overran and she was left to finish off because the SR had a meeting with sir himself at five and there were still two patients left to go.

One was a simple follow-up of a hip replacement which had clearly been a roaring success, and she had no trouble at all with it. The other, however, was more of a problem.

The patient was a young man with recurrent knee problems following a twisting injury in rugby the previous winter, over a year ago.

'It keeps locking,' he told her, 'and when it does I can't straighten it again for ages. Sometimes it takes days before it unlocks—usually at night, while I'm asleep—and when it goes it hurts like hell.'

Frankie gently flexed and extended the knee, rocking the joint and testing for any abnormal movement, but there was none, pointing to a meniscal tear rather than any ligament injury.

His X-rays seemed normal because the meniscus was cartilage and not radio-opaque, so it didn't show up on radiographs.

'I think we'd better put you down for arthroscopy, so we can have a look inside and see what's wrong. It can be done as a day case, if you like, or you might prefer to come in and spend about three days in hospital. You can return to work within a week or two—what do you do?'

'I'm a lorry driver—so you can see I need my legs for my work.'

She nodded thoughtfully. 'Do you have to load or unload the lorries?'

He grinned. 'No chance. Damn great container lorries—it's all done by cranes. I have to climb up into the cab, though, and change gear.'

'You'll need a fortnight off, then, I expect. Can you come in at any time?'

'Yes—whenever. You call, I'll take the time off. It's a big firm—they can juggle rotas if I give them a day or two's notice. They quite often have to cover for me without notice as it is, because I lock up without warning and then I can't work till it settles down again.'

She nodded again. 'OK, we'll put you down for the end of March, but if we get a cancellation before then we might call you in at the last minute, if you can manage that?'

'Brilliant,' he said with a grin, and swung his legs down off the couch. As he stood up and twisted round to pick up his trousers there was a dull creak and he gasped and fell against the couch.

'Damn! Blasted thing's gone again!'

She helped him into a chair, examined him again and found the knee joint locked solid, bent at a slight angle and unable to straighten or bend any more.

'Do you know what?' she said, eyeing him thoughtfully as he clutched it and winced. 'I think you should come in now and get that fixed tomorrow.'

He blinked at her. 'Can you do that?'

She shrugged. 'You're here, and it's causing you considerable distress—I can always admit you as an emergency. I'd better check with Mr Ryder, though, first. Just hang on here a minute.'

She didn't really want to speak to him. God knows how he would be with her after their skirmish at lunch-time, but Paul Redhill had to come first. She went through to the office, picked up the phone and got the switchboard to page him. He answered after a few seconds, and, putting their last conversation firmly out of her mind, she quickly outlined the patient's prob-lems and current situation.

'I'll come down; David and I have just about finished,' he told her, and the line went dead.

He appeared after a few minutes, examined the knee briefly, checked the notes and nodded.

'I think you ought to come in tonight. Is there any-one who could bring your things in?'

He nodded. 'My wife—she's outside in the waiting room.'

'Right. I'll have a word with her and we'll get you admitted ready for surgery in the morning. All right?'

He grinned, looking a little stunned. 'Great—if I'm not queue-jumping?'

Robert shook his head. 'It's a quick, simple pro-cedure that will get you back to work in good condition very quickly. As far as I'm concerned you're just as urgent a case as anybody else, possibly more so. I don't want my taxes wasted on you languishing at home!'

They both laughed, then Robert called Paul's wife and children in, explained the problem and then dropped the bombshell.

'Dr Bradley here will operate tomorrow and remove the loose fragment.'

She will? Frankie thought in horror. She had done very little keyhole surgery, and the thought of messing up this young man's knee frightened her to death. She almost wished she'd sent him home. At least by the end of March she might well have finished alienating Robert and have moved on. That way the man would have stood a chance of not losing the use of his knee—

'Dr Bradley, could I have a word?' Robert was saying.

'Sure.' She followed him into the office, shut the door and waited.

'Um—I just wanted to apologise.'

She blinked. 'You did?'

His grin was rueful and did funny things to her heart. 'I did. Look, can we get this chap sorted out and then go back to your room for a chat?'

'You just want my cake,' she accused, humour lurking in her voice along with a huge and unreasonable relief.

'Damn, you guessed,' he said softly, and the accompanying smile touched his eyes and drove away the bleakness, just for a heartbeat.

'I'll go up to the ward and clerk him afterwards. We'll get a porter to take him up and then go and put the kettle on. All right?' Frankie said.

'Sounds good to me.'

They exchanged a smile, and while Frankie made the admission arrangements Robert went over again with Mr Redhill the exact procedure for the morning and precisely what they hoped to achieve.

The door between the two rooms was slightly ajar, and Frankie heard their patient say, 'This Dr Bradley—she has done this sort of thing before, hasn't she?'

Frankie held her breath, then almost laughed aloud at Robert's devious cheek.

'Oh, she's an excellent surgeon. I was really lucky to get her; she's worth her weight in gold. Her surgical techniques are outstanding.'

Outstanding, indeed. She'd have to take him up on

that. She picked up the phone, contacted the ward and prepared them for Mr Redhill's admission, then called the porter's lodge.

A very few moments later Alvin arrived, whistling cheerfully and slightly off-key, and took Mr Redhill up to the ward in a wheelchair, his wife and children in attendance.

Frankie eyed Robert across the consulting room with a cynical grin.

'Outstanding, eh?'

He grinned. 'What else could I say? Actually she's never done this before, but don't worry, you've always got the other leg?'

She chuckled. 'I suppose not, but you didn't have to exaggerate.'

His grin faded. 'Actually,' he told her seriously, 'I didn't. They are quite outstanding. Your last firm thought a great deal of you, Frankie. I had a long chat with your old boss after I offered you the job. He was very sorry to see you go.'

She felt the warm flush of pleasure brush her cheeks and turned away, tidying the desk and stacking the notes on the secretary's desk ready for filing in the morning.

'Frankie?'

'Mmm?' She tidied furiously.

'I wouldn't let you do it if I didn't think you were ready.'

'I think you're a bit ahead of me,' she said with a nervous laugh.

'Nonsense.' He laid a hand over hers. 'Those pencils are straight, Frankie,' he said gently.

She shoved her hands in the pockets of her coat and straightened up with a bolstering sigh.

'Tea and cake?' she suggested, her voice unnaturally bright.

'Good idea—because I still have to apologise and explain my behaviour.'

Oh, Lord, she had forgotten that.

They walked back to her room in a strange, expectant silence which persisted until they were sitting down, tea in hand and the cake tin lying on the bed between them.

Then Robert sighed and leant back against the wall, rolling his head on his shoulders as if his neck ached and he was tired.

He *was* tired. She could see that in the shadows under his eyes and the deep lines that bracketed his mouth. He looked drawn, worried—and in need of love.

Frankie's soft heart ached for him. He was so alone, coping with his flighty and senseless ex-wife and their sweet daughter, desperate to please and so unsure of herself. She wanted to wrap her arms round him and tell him it was all right, Jane would be fine and everything would settle down again.

She moved the cake tin out of the way and his eyes opened.

'Don't I get cake?' he murmured, his voice a little husky.

She smiled. 'Of course you get cake, but you need a hug first.'

She knelt beside him, facing him, and held out her arms. He didn't move, watching her steadily. 'How can you want to do that when I said what I did?'

She sat back on her heels and dropped her arms. 'You were worried about your daughter. If you thought I was a threat to her, of course you'd defend her.'

'I didn't really think you could be gay.'

'I don't care if you did or not. That isn't an insult. It's the fact that you thought I might have used Jane—for whatever reasons. . .money, influence, sex—that's what hurt. That you thought, even for a moment, that I could hurt a child or use her for my own ends.'

'You don't understand. . .' he began, and then ground to a halt, his mouth tight.

She laid a hand on his knee. 'So why don't you tell me?'

He sighed, closed his eyes and ran his hand down his face as if he could wipe away the past, but it was still there when he opened his eyes, haunting them.

'Jackie, my ex-wife, has a—how can I put it?— liberal attitude to sex. It got us into trouble when we were little more than kids, but for a while it was OK. We got married as soon as we found out she was pregnant, when I was twenty-one and she was nineteen.

'She was a nurse, I had just started my clinical training and I was in no position to support her or look after her. By the time I was doing my house year three years later she was stuck at home in a dingy flat with a difficult toddler and no money for anything, and not surprisingly she rebelled.

'She started running up bills on her credit card, getting her hair highlighted and buying expensive clothes, and she started nightclubbing while I was sleeping in at the hospital. She would get a babysitter or leave JJ with friends and go out for the night, coming back in the morning and picking her up and dropping her off at playschool, then going home to sleep.

'One night I was ill with flu and I went home, to find the place deserted. It was like the *Mary Celeste*— plates on the table, toys on the floor in the sitting room and no one there. I was frantic. I rang the hospital, our friends and finally her old flatmate Lu. She told me she had JJ, and that Jackie had gone out for a drink.'

He had his cup in a death grip, and Frankie eased it out of his hands and put it down.

'What happened then?'

He gave a harsh laugh. 'She came home, complete with that night's stud. He took one look at me and fled, and I hit the roof. That was when she told me she'd been meeting men at the nightclubs and going back with them to our flat for months.'

'So what did you do?'

'I told her if it happened again I'd throw her out and divorce her. I started staying at home as much as possible, taking her out whenever I could, but I just couldn't bring myself to touch her again after what she'd done.'

He laughed without humour. 'That was probably my greatest mistake. Jackie needs sex like the rest of us need food and water, and she just wasn't getting it from me. I came home from work one day to find she'd gone off with one of her lovers, taking JJ with her. I had no idea where they were, but one day the bailiffs turned up and took everything that didn't belong to the landlord. That was when I found out about the credit cards.'

He studied his fingers thoughtfully, and Frankie suppressed the urge to reach out and stroke back his hair and comfort him. How had it felt to be so badly treated, to have his daughter whisked away with no idea where she was and be left with a backlog of debts and gossip?

'She turned up about six months later, broke and unhappy, and begged me to have her back. I refused, but I found her a flat, got JJ into a school and started paying her bills. I got a job up here about two years ago, and because I couldn't see so much of JJ and didn't trust Jackie to look after her properly if I wasn't around I sent her to boarding school, with the strict proviso that when JJ was around there were no men on the scene.'

He snorted. 'Unfortunately she's not very good at complying with conditions. Every now and then she gets fed up and comes up to Suffolk and pleads with me, because I've got a house she wouldn't mind living in and a lifestyle she fancies—she says it's the only reason she married me in the first place, but when I point out that if it was that important perhaps she should have stuck it out she gets the sulks.

'But this business with the drugs—it's the last straw. Not only has she had her current lover round during the holidays, but I gather from JJ he even offered her a smoke.'

Frankie squeezed his leg reassuringly. 'She's too sensible.'

'Thank God.' He looked up at her, his eyes empty and lost. 'So now she's my responsibility, and I'm scared to death that I'll fail her.'

'You won't. How could you? You love her, and that's what she needs—love and reassurance. Friends will come with time, and I meant what I said. I'll happily take her shopping and spend time with her when I'm free.'

'But what about your own family? Don't you want to see them?'

She thought of Jeff and his bride, tucked up in the Victorian house she had helped to renovate and had thought of as home, and smiled gently. 'They don't need me any more.'

'I do,' he told her. Their eyes locked, and for a moment she wasn't sure of his meaning. Then he added, 'At least, Jane does,' and the breath eased out of her lungs in a sigh of—disappointment?

'Sheet-lightning', he'd said. She backed away from the cloud.

'And I'm here for her,' she said firmly. 'Now, since we've got that out of the way, how about some cake while you tell me about Mr Redhill's knee and how I'm going to have to do this operation?'

He nodded and stood up, rummaged through her orthopaedic textbooks and found the most appropriate, then flicked through it while he munched the cake she handed to him.

'Here—this is what we're looking at—a tear in the medial meniscus. Now with the arthroscope we can see inside the knee and find the offending flap, cut it off and pull it out through tiny holes that will leave the knee virtually untouched. The difficult bit is deciding how much to cut off, because you want to leave the cushion of cartilage as intact as possible.'

'So how much will I have to take out?' she asked worriedly.

He shrugged. 'We won't know until you go in. There's probably a loose bit, too. Don't worry, I'll be there, watching it on the screen and guiding you. It's easy with practice.' He eyed the cake tin hopefully. 'Any more?'

'If you promise not to terrify me tomorrow by ignoring me like you did today.'

'What? When did I ignore you?'

She laughed. 'When I was doing the second hip replacement. I kept looking to you for guidance, and all you did was chat to the anaesthetist about Oliver Henderson's weekend crisis.'

'I was watching you all the time,' he objected. 'Just because I wasn't hovering over you like a neurotic fairy godmother, it doesn't mean I wasn't paying attention.'

That was true. He had jumped on her for the angle of the cup, and the rotation of the shaft, *and* for making too wide a slot for the shaft, so he must have been paying attention. 'OK,' she conceded. 'But I really am worried about the arthroscopy.'

'You shouldn't be telling me that,' he teased. 'You

should be telling me that of course you can cope and boning up on it the second my back's turned.'

'I'm not like that,' she said quietly. 'I'll do anything I'm confident to do, and whatever I do I do as well as I can, but I won't tackle something I'm not sure about. It isn't fair to the patient.'

His mouth softened. 'I wouldn't ask you to. Don't get defensive, Frankie. You're doing much better than I expected.'

She couldn't resist it. 'Better than you would have expected your other applicant to do?' she popped in.

He grinned. 'At least as well.' He glanced at his watch. 'You ought to go and clerk Paul Redhill, and I ought to be getting home and sorting out some arrangements for Jane. I'll need a nanny for half-term in a few weeks.'

Frankie chuckled as she put her cup in the basin in the corner. 'Don't call it a nanny in Jane's hearing— and do you really need one? Perhaps she's got school-friends she can go and stay with, at least for part of the time.'

'I'll ask.' He stood up, brushing crumbs off his lap, and put the plate down next to the empty cake tin. 'We finished it,' he said mournfully.

'I'll make another one with Jane this weekend,' she promised. 'That is, if you don't mind? I haven't got a proper kitchen here.'

'Of course I don't mind. I'd be delighted.' He hesitated near the door.

'Something wrong?' she murmured.

'Yes—drastically. I didn't get my hug,' he complained, humour touching his sad, lonely eyes.

'Poor baby,' she crooned, and, putting her arms round him, she squeezed gently, loving the feel of his warm, solid body under her hands. Oh, it felt so good to hold him like this, she thought as she ran one hand tenderly down his spine. He dropped his head onto her shoulder and sighed, his arms loose around her, pressing into the small of her back and easing her gently closer.

'Thank you for offering to help with Jane,' he murmured. 'I'm sorry I was so suspicious.'

'Idiot,' she said gently, and tipped her head back as he lifted his so that she could look him in the eye. 'She's a lovely girl. I know it may not always seem like that, but you're really very fortunate to have her.'

His smile was slow and sad. 'I know. I tell myself that all the time, whenever things get tough or complicated. That's what love's all about, isn't it? Being fortunate enough to have someone to care for, someone who needs you.'

His eyes dropped to her mouth, and they filled with hunger and a kind of desperation. Her breath lodged in her throat, but she swore that this time she wasn't going to grab him and kiss him the way she had before. Let him make the first move. . .

'I must go,' he muttered, his voice strained, and his arms fell away and he stepped back away from her. 'I'll see you at eight tomorrow for the ward round before Theatre,' he told her, but he avoided her eyes and turned quickly, almost yanking the door open in his haste.

She watched him go, her heart full, and wondered if he would ever let her in to warm that cold place inside him that found an echo in her own lonely heart.

'That's it; if you move the arthroscope round you can see the image alter as you sweep across the inside of the joint. There, now, can you see the tear? Go a little closer.'

She eased the instrument deeper into the joint, staring fixedly at the screen and trying to relate what she was seeing to what her hand was doing.

'OK, that's fine,' he told her. 'Now, you can see the extent of the tear and if I move the leg slightly you can see how that flap would interfere with movement— There, can you see how it fouls the joint?'

'Yes—oh, yes! No wonder it locks!'

'That's not locking it,' he told her. 'There must be a loose fragment somewhere.'

She felt the warm, firm grip of his hand over hers, moving the arthroscope across in an arc, probing and searching until he found what he was looking for. 'There,' he said with satisfaction. 'That's the offending article.'

'So what do you remove?' she asked, trying to concentrate on the patient and not the feel of Robert's hand on hers.

'*You*,' he emphasised softly, 'will remove the loose fragment and trim off the flapping section of the meniscus, cutting it back so that it leaves a clean edge for the joint to ride on. You need to make another little incision here—' he indicated the position on the other side of the knee '—and insert the tongs to remove that little chap before we lose it again, and then we'll go back and trim in a moment.'

He talked her through the incision, the insertion of the forceps and removal of the little fragment of meniscus, and the trimming of the tear and removal of the piece she had cut off.

'Fine. Now I just want to tidy up that meniscus a little before we finish,' he murmured, and, taking the instruments with her hands still on them, he guided her through a finer paring and grading of the meniscus until he was happy with the end result. 'Excellent,' he said softly, and his warm breath teased against her cheek and did funny things to her insides.

She could feel his chest against her shoulders, the

firm muscles of his arms bracketing hers, and knew that if she moved back a fraction their bodies would touch from head to toe.

She moved the other way, conscious of the 'sheet-lightning' and the fact that, despite having been given every opportunity last night, he had walked away from a kiss. She wasn't going to push him. If he didn't want to know, who was she to force the issue?

As he released her and moved sideways their bodies brushed, and she heard a muttered oath as he turned away.

'Right, what's next?' he asked, and as the anaesthetist reversed the anaesthetic Robert strode out of the operating room, dropping the swinging door behind him.

'What's eating him?' the scrub nurse said to Frankie.

She could have told the girl, but she didn't think it was wise. 'I have no idea,' she offered harmlessly.

'Wife trouble again, I expect. That woman is a right royal pain in the tail.'

Were there no secrets? Frankie wondered. First the man in the pub, now the theatre nurse—did they all know his business?

'I couldn't say,' she answered, and, peeling off her gloves and mask, she followed him slowly out. He was in the rest room.

'Coffee?' he asked.

'Please.'

She perched on a chair and took the proffered cup, then watched as he dropped into another chair and sighed.

'Jane rang me last night. She wants to come home this weekend and bring a friend.'

'That's nice.'

He looked at her. 'I'm on call. I had to say no. I didn't think the other girl's parents would approve of them being in the house unattended for the whole weekend. She's going to try and go to the girl's instead.'

'She'll enjoy that,' Frankie told him, trying to cheer him up.

He shook his head. 'She feels rejected,' he muttered. 'Small wonder. Mother isn't fit to have her and I can't find time for her. What a mess.'

'She surely realises you have to work?'

'Oh, yes. It just always seems to get in the way between us.' He stirred his coffee idly, then paused. 'Are you doing anything tonight?'

She thought of her textbooks, then looked at his face, somehow vulnerable despite the pride and defensiveness.

'No, nothing important.'

'Fancy supper? Nothing elaborate, just a vegetable hotpot or something, a little reward for being a clever girl—and I promise not to make you wash up.'

She chuckled, as she was meant to. 'Sounds good.'

'Do you want me to pick you up?'

She shook her head. 'No, I can find my way.'

'Eight?'

'Fine.'

'You did a good job there, by the way. Very neat.'

She dragged her mind back to the operation she had just performed. 'It's quite tricky getting the hand-eye co-ordination right through the screen.'

'It's because the scale's different. Your hand moves a fraction and the picture changes drastically. Also we aren't used to seeing out of the ends of our fingers, and that's what you're talking about. Still, you did well, for a first attempt.'

She grinned ruefully. 'You had to qualify that, didn't you? You couldn't just leave me with the "you did well", could you?'

'Wouldn't want you to get swollen-headed, Dr
Bradley. Now, about the next case. That's a bit more
tricky.'

More tricky? she thought in panic. 'Are you
doing it?'

He smiled. 'I think so. It's an amputation for vascu-
lar degeneration in a diabetic. You can watch
and learn.'

'Thank God for that,' she muttered under her
breath, and, downing her coffee, she followed him out
of the room.

He was an excellent cook. The hotpot was lovely, rich
and tasty and served with fresh broccoli and baby car-
rots. The kitchen, moreover, was immaculate, and
there was no question of sitting in the drawing room.

He led her straight into the kitchen, sat her down
at the table with a glass of red wine then dished up
on the side, plonking a huge plateful down in front of
her and seating himself opposite behind an equally
laden plate.

'Cheers,' he said with a defiant grin, and she
chuckled and clinked her glass with his.

'Cheers yourself. Jane would be so disappointed
in you.'

He chuckled. 'JJ needs a bit more formality in her
life. She'd be happy to abandon it then.'

As he had, Frankie thought, eyeing the casual bottle-
green cords and comfy green and navy sweatshirt. A
far cry from the suit he wore for clinics and ward
rounds, and different again from the less elegant but
professional theatre pyjamas he wore for operating.
His shoes were soft suede desert-boots, and she had
a feeling that they would come off given the slightest
encouragement.

She had changed her image too, abandoning the

severe 'I'm a professional, take me seriously' skirts and blouses in favour of a soft knit dress that draped and swirled and made her feel feminine and sensuous. He hadn't commented on it, but she had felt his eyes on her with a curious womanly pride, and had swirled just a little more than was necessary.

She ate everything he put in front of her, sat tight as instructed while he loaded the last few things into the dishwasher and put it on, and then obediently followed him through into the snug family sitting room with the wonderful chairs and the cosy woodburner and lovely friendly ambience.

'Port?' he offered, and she noticed that the bottle had been opened.

'A little one; I have to drive.'

'Not yet, though. I'll make some coffee in a bit. Have a taste. It's wonderful; you'll enjoy it. One of my juniors gave it to me for my birthday—currying favour, or something. Works, too; it's wonderful stuff.'

She laughed softly. 'I was doing no such thing; I'm not like that.'

'I know. You're too generous for your own good. Here.' He handed her a glass which she was glad to see only contained a small measure, and raised his own. 'To a budding orthopaedic surgeon.'

She raised her glass. 'To an excellent teacher.'

Their eyes locked, and she sipped and choked. He took the glass from her, rubbed her back gently and then looked down into her swimming eyes. 'OK?'

'Mmm,' she croaked. 'Wrong way.'

He smiled absently and dabbed her eyes with a tissue. 'Jane says you've got lovely eyes,' he murmured.

'Jane?' Frankie said, her voice still squeaky.

'Mmm. She's right—they are quite, quite beautiful. . .'

There was a long, tremulous pause and then he

moved away with a tiny sigh and handed her back her glass.

'Here. Try again—carefully this time.'

'I will.' She slipped off her shoes, curled up in the chair and cautiously tasted the port. 'Oh, it is nice.'

'I said it was. You ought to believe me.' He sprawled out in the other chair, long legs stretched out towards the warmth of the fire, and sighed again.

'You sound tired,' she said softly.

'Tired? I suppose I am. Weary, more. I could do with a break—something exciting. A trip to Outer Mongolia or something.'

'Outer Mongolia?' she spluttered. 'In January?'

He grinned. 'Well, Bermuda, then. I don't know. Somewhere exotic.'

'How about Center Parcs?'

'You too?' he exclaimed. 'Are you all mad? Jane keeps on about that place—but anyway, the idea's fatally flawed. I said exotic.'

'Well, there's the subtropical swimming paradise—that's pretty exotic in January. There's even a hot salt pool that goes outside and you can swim in freezing rain in this wonderful hot, salty water. It's amazing. Jane's right—you'd love it.'

'Hardly. She might but *I* need the break,' he groaned.

'So does Jane,' Frankie argued, warming to her theme. 'She's had practically no time with you. It would be real quality time.'

'In January?' His voice was loaded with scepticism.

'It's wonderful. I went last year in November with a group of friends and it was absolutely fantastic. We had so much fun.'

'I'm unconvinced.'

She grinned. 'You would be. It's a sign of old age. How old were you last Friday?'

He glared at her. 'Thirty-five. That is not old.'

'Too old to ride a bike, though.'

He bristled visibly. 'I am not too old to ride a bike!'

'Or go down a water-chute?'

He closed his eyes. 'I can't bear it.'

'You'd love it. Go on, ring up and ask about it. Get a brochure.'

'I don't want to go,' he persisted.

She played her trump card. 'You owe it to Jane.'

His eyes opened and locked with hers. 'Damn you, Frances Bradley, that is a low, sneaky trick.'

She grinned. 'Go on, then. Ring up tomorrow.'

'If you think it's such a damn good idea, why don't you come with us?'

She searched his face. 'Is that an invitation?' she ventured finally.

He let his breath out on a rueful sigh. 'I do believe it might be,' he agreed.

She couldn't keep the smile in to save her life. 'You won't regret it,' she promised him fervently. 'You'll have the time of your life.'

His disbelieving snort was her only reply.

For eight years Robert had lived a solitary, tidy existence, unencumbered by romantic entanglements and the tender threads of love.

Now he found himself inviting a beautiful woman who played havoc with his blood pressure along on a weekend break with him and his daughter!

'I must be mad,' he muttered, watching the tail-lights of Frankie's car disappearing down the drive. He had refused to kiss her goodnight—well, nothing more than a brush on the lips that had hardly lingered for more than a heartbeat—but even so the sparks were flying and his pulse was racing.

Sheet-lightning? Nothing so innocuous. It was like

having a couple of pounds of Semtex in his trousers, and just now it felt as if it was about to go off.

A whole weekend of fun and frolics? He was going to have to watch her sashaying about in a tiny swimsuit the way she had in that delectable and very, very sexy dress, and keep his reaction firmly under control or die of embarrassment.

He supposed he could always spend the whole weekend in the cold-plunge pool. . .

CHAPTER FIVE

'So, HOW does it feel?' Robert asked.

'Oh, sore.' Paul Redhill gave them a wry smile. 'I wonder if it was actually that bad.'

'It was,' Robert assured him. 'The tear was quite significant, and we removed a piece which had detached and was causing the locking. You should find it a great deal better in a day or two. What pain medication is he on?' he asked, turning to Frankie.

'He's had pethidine overnight and he's on to slow-release dihydrocodeine and paracetamol now.'

Robert nodded. 'You should find that the pain wears off during the next day or two, but you must rest and take it very easy for a few days, then come back for a check-up this time next week and we'll go from there. Hopefully you'll be back at work in a fortnight, and it'll be as good as new in about six weeks. Sister O'Brien will make you an appointment, and then you can go home.'

They left his bedside and moved on, going to see Joseph Lee, the man with the old non-union of the tibia who had been knocked down in the early hours of New Year's Day on his way home from a party. His leg was making very slow progress, but the swelling had gone down, the wounds were closed and his foot was well—Robert's primary concern.

'How long will it be before we know if the bone will knit?' Mr Lee asked them.

'I don't know,' Robert told him honestly. 'Sometimes the process is very slow. We'll X-ray it again today and see how it looks at the moment, make sure the bones are well aligned and the fixators are doing their job properly, then we'll just keep a steady eye on it. Tell me,' he said, 'why wasn't the previous fracture followed up to make sure it had healed?'

'Well, it was and it wasn't,' he confessed. 'I should have gone back—I knew there was something not quite right, but I thought with time it would sort itself out.'

He laughed. 'Of course it didn't, but we moved and it meant seeing a new doctor, and so long as I used the crutches all the time it didn't really trouble me if I was careful, and I couldn't afford to take time off work. I'm self-employed, a clock-mender, setting up in business in a new place, and the wife's not well— we need the money.

'Still, it's out of my hands now, so maybe this time I'll get it sorted out. Of course we'll get quite a hefty whack from the driver's insurance, so I won't lose out.' He sighed. 'Trouble is, of course, these things take time and in the meantime we've got nothing coming in.'

'Is that a problem?' Robert asked.

'Well, it will be soon—and there's no one to look after my wife.'

'I'll get Sister O'Brien to contact the social services people. They have contingency plans for this sort of thing, so I'm sure they'll be able to help you in the short term. Have a word, anyway. And I think you could probably go home at the end of the week, pro-vided you promise faithfully to use your crutches without fail, rest the leg if it hurts and don't do too much. Do you work sitting down?'

'At a bench, yes.'

'Could you prop the leg up?'

He smiled. 'That's what I've been doing.'

'Then I don't see any reason why you can't continue. I'll sort out the paperwork and you can go home on

Friday provided today's X-rays are all right,' he told him.

Mr Lee smiled, hugely relieved. 'Thanks, Doc. That's such a weight off my mind.'

'You come back, though, for your check-ups,' he said warningly.

'I will—thanks.'

They moved on, Robert prompting Frankie to sort out the X-rays of Mr Lee's leg and discussing their next patient—young Darren Hawkes who had been knocked off his bike on New Year's Day and damaged his ankle.

'His foot seems to be recovering reasonably well, but he'll need skin grafts. I'll get him back to Theatre later today, I think, and we'll put a partial-thickness graft on. It's too extensive for a full-thickness.'

'It seems to have stabilised well,' Frankie said as they approached the bed. 'The wound looks much cleaner than I thought it would.'

'That's because we cleaned it out properly,' Robert reminded her.

'Even though I took too long?'

He grinned. 'You can't take too long doing a job like that. It takes as long as it takes. You did the right thing.'

More praise! Heavens, if he went on like this she'd end up with a permanent job, Frankie thought with a little mental chuckle. Wonders would never cease.

She spent her short lunch-break reading up about skin grafts, so by the time they went into Theatre that afternoon with Darren Hawkes she was well up on it. Theory and practice, though, she was to discover, were light years apart, and the dermatome—the tool used for harvesting the sliver of skin—simply refused to cooperate.

After her second attempt Robert took over, running the dermatome firmly and evenly over the donor site on the patient's abdomen and then using a special device to cut the skin all over into a sort of mesh, so that when he placed the first graft over the damaged tissues of the ankle it covered a far greater area than it otherwise would. 'Right, now try again,' he told her.

Again she struggled, but this time with rather more success, and she laid the second strip of skin beside the first with great satisfaction.

'Better. One more should do it. Use the other side of his abdomen,' he instructed.

She struggled again but this piece was less co-operative and by the time the ankle was covered in a mesh of new skin and the graft firmly bandaged on to encourage the skin to take she was hot, frustrated and not very satisfied with her performance.

She left the room, threw her gown and gloves into the bin and gave a sharp sigh of disgust.

'Well done,' Robert said from behind her.

'Well done'? What was he talking about? She shot him a disbelieving look and he smiled.

'It isn't easy. You did fine for a first attempt. You'll get better. Anyway, skin's remarkably forgiving. It has this wonderful ability to heal.'

'Good job,' she muttered, and, pouring herself a cup of coffee, she dropped into a chair and sighed again.

'Hey, chin up,' he murmured. 'You're too hard on yourself.'

'I'm a perfectionist,' she said tightly. 'He'll have scars.'

'Inevitably. That's hardly your fault, though.'

'They'll be worse than they need have been.'

'No, they won't. It will heal up and look fine—you'll see. OK, it'll be scarred, but not because of anything you've done. Possibly a plastic surgeon could have done a better job, but we're talking about functional use of the limb and reasonable cosmetic result, not entry to Mr Universe.'

She gave a rueful laugh. 'OK, but I still think I could have done it better.'

'Maybe with practice. You need to learn that it's all right to be only almost perfect some of the time. A little healthy criticism every now and then is fine, but you need to allow yourself your successes as well.'

She gave him a withering look. 'That was not a success.'

'Of course it was. Most of those grafts were fine.'

'But not all.'

'No. Surgery's like that. It was the skin and not you that was the problem with the last graft.

'By the way, Jane rang. Her friend's got chickenpox and has gone home, and so she's coming back here for the weekend on her own.'

Frankie watched him for a moment, struggling with his conscience, and then baled him out. 'I'd offer to cover for you here, but I don't think I can yet. If you like I'll take her shopping on Saturday. I could do with a bit of retail therapy after this week.'

He chuckled. 'Just bear in mind I have a limited budget.'

'Oh, so do I,' she said drily. 'I'll teach her to hunt up bargains and make them look expensive. Anyway, with that gorgeous willowy figure she could wear rags and look extravagant.'

'Hmm,' he murmured. 'Just like someone else I know.'

'Oh, no,' she demurred instantly and without thought. 'My bust's too big.'

'Not for me,' he said softly, and she felt the warmth of his approval flood her body in a sensuous tide.

Her breath caught in her throat and she looked

away, unable to meet those hot, hungry eyes. He swore softly under his breath and then apologised.

'I didn't mean to get personal,' he muttered. 'I'm sorry.'

She allowed a soft, womanly smile to brush her lips. 'Don't be. I'll take it as a compliment. Now, the next case—you or me?'

'Me, I think. Maybe concentrating on a patient will take my mind off you. How the hell you manage to look sexy in those ridiculous pyjamas I can't imagine, but you do, and it plays havoc with my blood pressure.'

And she had thought he was unaware of her! Her feminine pride blossomed. 'I'll keep very quiet,' she promised.

He snorted. 'I doubt it. It's not in your nature. I expect you were born asking questions.'

She giggled. 'Me? I expect I was. I know they were all fed up with me by the time I went to school, and then it got worse because I kept asking questions about what I'd done that day. They'd had enough by the time I was eleven, and when I got a scholarship they sent me to boarding school to drive the teachers mad!'

'I'm sure you did,' he said drily, but his eyes were laughing and for once the bleak loneliness was missing. Frankie felt her heart surge with—what? Love? Dear God, it felt very like it. It was certainly more than the simple urge to rescue lame ducks that she'd had since she was tiny.

That was the other thing that had driven her family mad, she recalled. Were her feelings for Robert just an extension of that, or something more, something deeper and more significant?

'Penny for them.'

'No fear.' She stood up. 'Come on, then, let's go and look at the case-notes and X-rays, and you can talk me through it while I try not to ask too many questions.'

The rest of that week provided her with plenty of opportunities to ponder on her feelings for Robert. For whatever reason, he had taken her under his wing, working with her almost all the time. She knew it must mean that he dealt with paperwork in the evenings instead of the day, and often when she passed his office in the evening she would find the light on.

Sometimes he would come up to the ward and discuss a case with her, or oversee her admission of new patients and go over the plates with her.

All of it, she knew, was above and beyond the call of duty and she couldn't work out the reason for it. Either he didn't trust her an inch, and from his praise that seemed unlikely, or else he was just finding excuses to be near her.

She found that possibility nearly as unlikely as the first, but bearing in mind his admission that he found her sexy in theatre pyjamas, and bearing in mind also the look in his eyes every time he nearly but not quite kissed her, she thought it the most likely option.

In which case, she realised, it was quite likely that they would end up having an affair, and since she didn't believe in leaving matters like that to chance she enrolled with a GP and went on the Pill. The last thing he needed, she reasoned, was another child conceived out of wedlock.

On Friday morning they had a routine fracture clinic, and for once he left her alone, taking the other half of the patients for himself and working in a separate room. Nevertheless he was there in the event of a problem, and when one patient came in shortly before the end of the clinic she was glad he was about.

She watched the patient limp towards her and had a sudden, gut feeling that she would need Robert, even before she went any further. The man was young, about her age or a little younger, and from his appearance she realised that he was one of life's unfortunates. His clothes were ragged, his eyes empty, and apart from the relatively clean plaster cast on his right wrist he was filthy.

She glanced at his notes, and saw under the section for his address 'NFA'—no fixed abode. It figured. He had the helpless, wary look of the homeless, defensive and yet so vulnerable.

She gave him a welcoming smile. 'Come in, Mr Pate. I gather you slipped on the ice and broke your wrist yesterday—how is it feeling?'

'All right, really. Bit sore off and on.'

'I'm sure. Can you move your fingers for me?'

'Sort of—it hurts a bit.'

'That's fine.' She turned the wrist over and examined the outside of the fracture site for swelling, while her mind toyed with the disparity between Mr Pate's relatively cultured voice and his appearance and lack of address. What twist of fate had brought him to this point in his life? she wondered.

She laid his hand gently down on the couch and smiled at him. 'Good, that's lovely. Right, well, as it doesn't seem to be too swollen I think you can have the proper plaster on it now and then we'll see you again in a couple of weeks. You were lucky; it's only a hairline crack.' She glanced at the notes. 'I see your leg isn't mentioned in the notes. Did you hurt it at the same time?'

He looked surprised. 'My leg? No, that was years ago. I got in a brawl and someone kicked me, and—well, it's never really been right since.'

She frowned. 'Have you seen a doctor about it?'

He snorted. 'They won't make house calls where I have to live, Doctor.'

'Where are you living at the moment?' she probed gently.

'In an old warehouse by the river. Not for long, though. The developers are coming in in a few weeks and turning it into bijou little apartments for would-be yuppies.'

She was startled yet again by his voice and turn of phrase. He was clearly educated, and yet living rough. What had gone wrong?

'How about enrolling with a GP?' she asked, trying to stick to the point.

He snorted. 'They don't like it when we go in. I tried to see one once, and the receptionist turned me away. Said I smelt. She'd bloody well smell if she lived where I do.'

Frankie, who had been trying not to notice the smell, changed the subject back to his leg. 'So, what's the problem with your leg?' she asked.

'Well, it sort of oozes—stinking stuff—and sometimes little splinters come out—I think it's bone but I'm not sure. Odd, really.'

Very odd. Frankie asked him to slip his trousers off and climb on the couch, and when she looked at his shin she was horrified. It was a textbook case of chronic osteomyelitis, with a discharging sinus and probably a large chunk of dead bone inside, trapped within a new layer of living bone that was desperately trying to evict the dead matter.

'I think we need some X-rays of that, and then we'll have a word with the consultant, I think, Mr Pate. I'll get a porter to take you through to X-Ray in a chair. Hang on.'

She sorted out the X-ray requests, sent him off for the pictures and, with a quick spray of air freshener, called in the next patient, dealt with what turned out to be a very straightforward eight-week check on a broken arm and sent the patient away castless and content.

If only they were all so easy, she thought, and, collecting the X-rays from the clip on the wall, she took them through into her room and examined them. There, sure enough, was a clearly visible lump of dead bone inside a rather ragged-looking tibia.

'Bingo,' she said in satisfaction, and, tugging the plates off the light box, she went through to Robert just as he was finishing with a patient.

'Can I show you this?' she asked, and snapped them up onto his light box.

'Good Lord. Chronic osteomyelitis. Have you been raiding the archives?'

She smiled. 'No—twenty-six-year-old patient, no fixed abode, with history of a kick to the leg some years ago, no medical attention, says it oozes and sometimes bits of bone come out.'

'Lovely.'

'It is. You'd better see it; it's way beyond my experience.'

He laughed. 'Mine too, I expect.'

He followed her back, examined the leg carefully and then stood back, arms folded, and stared at the young man. 'It must be sore,' he said.

'It hurts more sometimes than others. The cold is pretty grim.'

'Well, I think we ought to deal with it fairly promptly. Is there any reason why you can't come into hospital now?'

He looked stunned. 'For the leg?'

'Yes. You have a condition where the bone has been injured—by a kick in your case—and because it bleeds round under the membrane that covers the bone that section of bone dies. The membrane then makes a new bone over the top, but the dead bone is trapped inside. Your new bone is trying to get rid of it, hence the discharge from the hole on your shin and the bits of bone that come out.

'Unfortunately it'll take more than your lifetime to get the rest of that bone out, so what we need to do is open it up, remove the dead and diseased bone, clear up the infection and once it's all free of bugs we can put a bone graft back in from another part of your body—your hip, for example—and then hopefully it will heal up properly and you'll be able to walk again without pain, and certainly without a leaky, smelly hole in your leg.'

'However long does that take?' he asked with a little frown.

'Possibly three months? You'll have to be on the antibiotics for longer—maybe even up to a year, to be on the safe side.'

He shook his head. 'And I thought it was just a bit of a nuisance. I never realised all that was going on inside.' He gave a little chuckle. 'Oh, well, I suppose it gets me a warm bed for the rest of the winter. Can't be all bad, eh?'

Frankie laughed softly. 'The lengths some people will go to. I'll need some blood from you for culture so we can find the germ that's causing it, and then we need to start the drug treatment, I imagine.'

She looked to Robert for advice and he nodded. 'I think ampicillin and flucoxacillin, both 500 mg four times a day, but not until we've got the blood safely out and in the lab, because I'd hate to be treating the wrong thing. You could also take a swab of the sinus and see what the pus contains. OK? If you admit Mr Pate now I'll see him on the ward this afternoon.'

'Uh—could I go back to my place and pick up my

things? There's not much, but it's all I've got. I'd like to hang onto it if I could.'

'How long will it take you?' Robert asked.

He shrugged. 'Two hours?'

Robert nodded. 'Fine. Go and sort yourself out while we get your admission all organised and then come back into the orthopaedic ward as soon as you're ready.

'Oh, Dr Bradley, take the blood first, and the swabs, so the lab can get them under way—then I think a case conference over lunch, OK?'

She nodded, unsure whether he wanted the lunch or the case conference, and unsure whether even he knew. 'I'll see you in the canteen in a few minutes,' she told him, and then turned back to her patient. 'Now, if you could roll up your left sleeve for me I'll do my leech bit and we'll get a swab off that leg, and then you can go. We'll put the fresh cast on your arm when you're back in—we can do that on the ward. That's lovely.'

She drew up the blood, labelled the bottles and sent them off with a porter then made her way down to the canteen. Robert was there waiting, and greeted her with a wave. She made her way over to his table and found a selection of filled rolls and two cups of coffee.

'Is this OK?'

'Sure—what's the case conference about?'

He gave a wry grin. 'Did I say anything about a case conference? I just wanted to see you before tomorrow, to sort out what's happening. We're on take, and I wanted to make sure you're happy about covering tonight while I go and fetch Jane from school in Cambridge. I'll be gone about two hours.'

'I should think so—is David about?'

'Unfortunately not. He should have been, but his

father's ill and he wanted to go home for the weekend. I knew you and Jane would want to do girly things all weekend, so I thought I might as well work. Oh, and by the way, I've book Center Parcs for next weekend. We're both off duty—or we are now. The other firm's on take, and Nick Davidson can cover any problems with our patients. Is that OK?'

She thought of the whole weekend spent with him and Jane, laughing and having fun and doing things together like a family, and a huge well of happiness surged up inside her. 'Sounds wonderful,' she told him, and she didn't care if her eyes were shining and her heart was on her sleeve.

For a long moment he stared at her, his mouth opening as if he was going to say something, and then he closed it and with a visible effort looked away. 'Eat up,' he said with forced cheer. 'You've got a ward full of patients waiting to go home and a whole lot more all ready to break something and come in. You need your strength.'

He pushed the plate towards her and she took a roll, sinking her teeth into it and wondering when they were going to get onto this wonderful, exciting roller coaster that beckoned. Because one thing was for sure: it couldn't be long. . .

The night was longer than she would have thought possible.

She was up for half of it, covering emergencies and little run-of-the-mill problems like patients who couldn't sleep and post-op pain relief that wasn't working adequately, and by Saturday morning she was feeling tired, frayed and more than ready to hand over the bleeper to Robert and run.

Romance was the last thing on her mind, and when she drove up outside his house she was feeling less than her best. However, Jane came out and wandered over, looking awkward, and so with a dredged-up smile she climbed out of the car, slammed the door and walked briskly towards the girl.

'Ready for the major shopping trip of the century?' she said with a grin.

'Do you really want to take me?' Jane ventured tentatively.

Frankie shot her a look. 'Actually I was thinking more in terms of going with you rather than taking you. I want to try some new things on, and it's so difficult without someone to tell you if things work for you. I don't suppose I'm exactly your idea of fun, but I could certainly use some advice if you wouldn't mind, and I'm happy to return the favour.'

Jane gave her a shy smile. 'I don't mind at all, and I've got hardly any clothes that fit because I've grown miles this year.' She pulled a face. 'Dad says I'm not to bankrupt him.'

Frankie chuckled. 'Don't worry, we'll be sensible. Is he inside?'

'Yes—eating breakfast. He didn't sleep very well. He said to offer you a coffee before I dragged you off to town.'

'Sounds good.' She followed Jane inside, and found Robert slumped over the kitchen table reading the paper, a steaming mug of coffee in his hand.

He looked up as they went in and searched her face. 'Hi. How was it? You didn't call me.'

She laughed. 'Is that why you had a bad night—wondering if the phone was out of order? I didn't call because I didn't need to.'

'A likely story. Jane, go and do your homework for a little while, darling, please. Coffee?'

'Lovely.' She sat down at the table, turned the paper round and scanned it idly.

'I was reading that,' he complained, turning it back again, and then folded it up and grimaced at her. 'If you must know I spent the night worrying about whether you would cope.'

She shook her head reproachfully. 'I would have rung you, you know that. I don't do things I can't cope with.'

'Nor do I—which is why it's you and not me taking Jane shopping!' He eyed her thoughtfully. 'Frankie, are you sure you want to do this?'

She laughed. 'Why is it that men hate shopping so much they can't imagine anyone doing it for fun?'

'Fun?' He shuddered. 'You must be mad. However, don't let me put you off, because she desperately needs new things. Here—' he handed her a wad of notes '—that should start you off. If you run out, here's my cashpoint card. If I tell you the number will you remember it?'

She stared at him in amazement. 'You're very trusting.'

'Shouldn't I be?'

'Don't be silly. Write it on my arm. I'd hate my defective memory to curtail Jane's fun!'

He rolled his eyes and wrote the number on her forearm in ballpoint pen. 'While you're in the shops, can you get her some new underwear? She's growing up so fast I'm sure it won't still fit, but it's not really something I can ask her.'

'Don't worry,' she said with a reassuring smile. 'I'll sort her out. Leave it with me—and I promise not to bankrupt you.'

In the event she didn't—not quite! Jane tried on garment after garment, with Frankie ruthlessly rejecting things that didn't suit her or looked cheap or were inferior quality, weeding out the things that would be difficult to look after, until in the end they had a basic wardrobe of good, easy-care casual clothes that suited her tall, slender frame and still allowed for expansion in necessary areas.

On that subject they found some pretty bras with more support than her first ones, now hopelessly out-grown, and some matching lace-trimmed briefs that made more allowance for the gentle swell of her hips.

They finished off with a pair of boots and some trainers, and then Jane looked expectantly at Frankie. 'Your turn,' she said with a grin.

Frankie groaned. 'Let's have a cup of tea first. It's hours since lunch.'

It wasn't, but the previous night was taking its toll and her legs were aching, her head was throbbing and she really didn't feel like worrying about herself. The tea refreshed her, though, and as they wandered back through the shopping mall a dress caught her eye.

'That would suit you,' Jane said immediately, pointing out the same dress.

It was very simple, a long-sleeved, figure-skimming jersey knit made of pure silk, nubbly but unbelievably soft and comfortable, in a lovely smoky green that warmed her complexion and did wonderful things to her hair.

She pulled it on then stood back.

'Oh, wow,' Jane said breathlessly.

Frankie turned sideways and eyed herself critically. Too busty, she thought, and then remembered Robert's remark. 'Not for me,' he'd said, and she felt the glow of his approval all over again.

'I'll have it,' she decided, and didn't even wince at the price. It would be worth it just to see that look in his eyes again.

'Right, young lady, I've had enough,' she announced once she'd paid, and, gathering up all their parcels, they made their way back to the car.

Robert arrived back just as they did and helped them with the bags, groaning dramatically. 'Do I need to go and rob a bank?' he asked Frankie, with a wince, and she laughed.

'Absolutely not. I didn't need your cashpoint card, and you've even got some change.'

He looked astonished. 'I have? Good God. Let's see everything, then.'

Jane ushered them into the kitchen, took the parcels one at a time into the sitting room next door and treated them to a fashion show.

Robert's face was a sea of emotions—pride, love and a certain confusion that his little girl could have grown up so much so fast.

'She looks beautiful,' he said softly to Frankie.

'She is beautiful, when she hasn't got that stroppy, defensive look on. We've had a really lovely day, haven't we, Jane?' she said as the girl came back in, dressed in her new leggings and long, stripey cotton cardigan.

'Brilliant. What's for supper? I'm starving.'

Robert gave a rueful grin. 'I guess she is hungry, doing all that growing. What's in these bags?'

'Oh, undies,' Jane said, snatching up her last two bags. 'That's Frankie's. Frankie, go and put it on and give us a twirl.'

'Oh, no; you don't want to see it.'

'Yes, we do,' they chorused.

She went, because it would have created more fuss not to, and tugged the dress on, dragging her trembling fingers through her hair to restore it to some semblance of order, then, swamped with a sudden attack of nerves, she went back into the kitchen.

'There,' Jane said with pride, 'Doesn't she look wonderful?'

Robert was silent for a moment, then he told her to turn round. His voice was husky, and after she had done a slow twirl she met his eyes.

It was a wonder she didn't catch fire.

'Well?' Jane persisted. 'Doesn't she look gorgeous? Dad, say something.'

He cleared his thoat. 'Beautiful,' he rasped, and cleared his throat again. 'I think it deserves an occasion,' he said, his voice almost back to normal. 'David's back—his father's all right—so he's covering the rest of the weekend. Stay for dinner. Let me cook for you, to thank you for taking Jane to town and just so you've got an excuse to keep the dress on.'

Frankie's shyness evaporated, driven out by the warmth in his eyes and the slow beat of desire in her veins.

'Thank you,' she murmured, and her own voice was slightly husky, echoing with countless generations of a need as old as time.

'So are you staying?' Jane asked.

'Yes, she is,' Robert answered, his eyes still fixed on Frankie's.

'Great.' His daughter, oblivious to the tension running between them, picked up the bags and stuffed them in the bin, gathered up her clothes and ran lightly upstairs, humming softly. Seconds later they heard music flooding from her room, and a door banged shut in the distance.

Their eyes still locked, Robert murmured, 'I want to kiss you, but I daren't because I won't be able to stop.'

Frankie smiled tauntingly. 'You'd better not, then, had you?'

'No, I'd better not—not yet.'

*   *   *

He didn't, not for hours, not until Jane was long in bed and Frankie stood up to go. Then he did, moving until she was just touching him, his hands finding hers and clasping them lightly, his mouth lowering to settle against hers like the wing of a moth.

'I want you,' he sighed against her lips, and her breath locked in her throat. Her tongue flicked out to moisten her lips and brushed his, and with a ragged groan he slanted his mouth over hers and kissed her as if he were dying and she were the only cure.

She felt his hands settle on her hips, easing her closer, and then one hand slid up to cup the fullness of her breast. A groan rose in his throat and his fingers tightened slightly on the tender, swollen flesh that ached for his touch.

She leant into him, feeling the hard thrust of his desire and the shaking need that racked him, and her body ached to know him, to tear away the clothes that separated them and lie naked against him. She wanted the contrast between her smooth softness and the hard, taut lines of his body, wanted to feel her tender, dewy skin and the hair-roughened texture of his scraping gently against each other, dragging her relentlessly towards fulfilment.

Then they heard a door bang upstairs, and with a ragged sigh Robert released her and stepped back.

'I didn't mean to do that,' he said rawly. 'I wasn't going to touch you.'

She reached out and laid her fingers against his jaw, loving the feel of the harsh stubble against her skin. 'I'm glad you did,' she whispered.

'So am I.' He turned his mouth into her hand and kissed it, then folded her fingers over the kiss to trap it inside. 'Go home, Cinderella, before I ravish you and you turn into a pumpkin.'

She laughed softly. 'I think you've got your panto-mime in a muddle.'

'I don't wonder,' he murmured, rueful laughter brushing his eyes. 'Go on, Frankie. Go home while I'm still prepared to let you.'

She went, and all the way back to the hospital she could feel the warm imprint of his hand against her breast, and she held the kiss in her palm until she fell asleep. . .

CHAPTER SIX

FRANKIE spent the whole of Sunday trying to forget about that kiss and reading everything she could find about chronic osteomyelitis—partly so that she would know as much as possible about it before Jim Pate's surgery on Monday, and partly to take her mind off Robert.

She'd hung the new dress at the back of the wardrobe—out of sight, out of mind, she reasoned—and, dressed in old leggings and a scruffy sweatshirt, she curled up on the bed with a heap of books and drifted in and out of fantasy for most of the afternoon.

Finally, despairing of herself, she went for a walk in the park near the hospital. It was a lovely afternoon, if rather cold, and she came back refreshed and ready to tackle the books with more enthusiasm.

There was a note under her door. 'Taking J. J. back to Cambridge—wondered if you wanted to come along for the ride. Phone before six. R.'

It was ten past five, and she chewed her lip and agonised for all of five seconds before ringing him. 'Sounds wonderful—I was reading about osteomyelitis, but you can tell me all about it instead on the way back,' she said with a laugh.

'Sounds riveting,' he replied drily. 'We'll pick you up in about an hour, OK?'

'Fine. I'll see you then.'

'Oh, and Frankie? Wear something sexless.'

She chuckled and put down the phone. Well, you couldn't get more sexless than her tatty leggings and thousand-year-old sweatshirt top, she thought, so just before six she brushed her hair, cleaned her teeth and found some shoes, then wandered out into the corridor.

Gavin Jones, the surgical registrar who had invited her out on the night of Robert's birthday, came out of the kitchen opposite and fell into step beside her. 'Hi,' he said with a grin. 'How's it going?'

'I'm still alive,' she said with a laugh. 'Still on trial—the worst is yet to come. We've got a chap in with chronic osteomyelitis—and apparently I get the pleasure,' she added drily.

He chuckled. 'Lucky you. Oh, well, you could be sitting in a grotty bedsit on social security.'

'Yes, and if I foul it up I may well be yet!'

They laughed together, and as they rounded the corner they nearly bumped into Robert coming towards them.

'Oh, hi,' she said with a smile, the laughter still in her voice, and then she saw his eyes, stormy and distant, and her smile slipped.

Gavin took one look at Robert's face and with a wave and a quick, 'I'll see you around, Frankie,' he carried on, leaving her with a glowering Robert.

She turned to him. 'What's wrong?'

'Nothing,' he retorted crisply. 'Are you ready?'

'Yes—if I'm OK like this?'

'Fine,' he replied. He didn't even look at her.

Well, she thought, what on earth is eating him? Another row with Jackie, perhaps? Or was Jane being awkward? Whatever, he wasn't going to be very good company all the way to Cambridge and back!

As they reached the door she put her hand on his arm and stopped him. 'Robert, are you sure you want me to come?'

'Don't you want to?' he asked shortly.

'Of course I want to—more to the point, I thought

you wanted me to. I just wondered if you'd thought better of it. You don't seem very pleased to see me.'

He looked at her then, his eyes still angry, and with a rough sigh he thrust his hands through his hair. 'I'm sorry. Actually I was wondering if you still wanted to come, or if you'd rather spend the evening with your friend.'

'Gavin?' she said with a little frown. 'No, of course not— Robert, are you jealous?'

He looked uncomfortable. 'Don't be silly. Why should I be jealous?'

She smiled gently. 'Because you don't want anybody else kissing me the way you did last night?' she murmured.

He swore softly. 'Damn it, Frankie, did you have to bring that up?' he growled.

She laughed, a little bubble of delight, and laid her hand on his arm. 'Come on, let's go,' she coaxed, and with a sigh he turned back towards the door and led her over to his car.

She sat in the back, letting Jane have her father to herself for the journey there. There would be plenty of time for them to sit together on the return journey, and anyway, from her position in the corner of the back seat she could watch him as he talked to Jane.

So he was jealous, she mused, and a centuries-old woman's smile curved her lips. How satisfying—not that there was anything to be jealous about, but at least it indicated a certain level of interest. She settled back and enjoyed the journey, and after he had taken Jane into school and settled Frankie in the front seat he slid behind the wheel, started the car and set off for home.

He said very little, and Frankie was quite happy listening to the music he put on. Then the tape finished and started again, and he flicked it out and handed it to her. 'Find something else,' he suggested, and she looked through the pile in the glove compartment and came up with a compilation album of love songs. Jane's, she thought, because they contrasted oddly with the rest of the collection.

She slipped the tape in, and they were instantly surrounded by soft, evocative music, husky voices and pleading words.

He shot her a questioning glance and she smiled, her face illuminated for a moment by the light spilling from the glove compartment until she closed it with a gentle snap.

'Damn it, Frankie, it's hard enough having to sit next to you looking like that without being surrounded by people crooning about loving and touching and God knows what,' he growled softly.

'Looking like what?' she said in surprise. 'I'm wearing ancient leggings and a sweatshirt that probably belonged to Mrs Noah!'

He sighed. 'You have no idea, have you, what you do to me? How I feel watching your body sway softly, the tempting thrust of your breasts, the little nubs of your nipples just crying out for the feel of my hand?' His voice was husky, rippling over her nerve-endings and leaving them exposed and trembling.

He held out his hand and she took it, pressing her lips to his palm before laying it flat against her thigh. He groaned and swerved, snatching his hand back and pulling off the road at the first junction.

They shot down a lane, off up another and finally he pulled over under a little group of trees and cut the engine. With a muffled curse he unfastened his seat belt and reached for her, his arms going round her and drawing her up against his chest as his mouth came down and locked with hers in a kiss that shook her to the centre of her being. Then it eased and became gentle, oh, so gentle, little sips and brushes and nibbles that made her whimper for more.

His hand, warm and firm, slid under her sweatshirt and found the catch of her bra, then the unbound fullness of her breasts spilled into his palm and he groaned aloud.

His mouth left hers, laying soft, moist kisses against the skin of her throat, down in the soft hollow where her pulse fluttered like a little bird, and then down again until she felt the tormenting flick of his tongue against her aching nipple.

With a little cry she arched against him and his mouth closed over her, drawing the tender nub into his mouth and sucking deeply.

She could have wept. Instead she bit her lip and cradled his head tenderly in her hands. Desire and love flooded through her, leaving her weak and vulnerable, aching for more. He shifted his attention to the other breast, caressing it with his tongue, his breath hot and yet cooling against the moist skin.

A little sob escaped her and he raised his head, his mouth returning to hers with a desperate hunger that matched her own. Then finally, when she was almost sobbing with need, he drew away and cradled her face in his hands, his thumbs soothing her fevered cheeks. 'Shh,' he murmured, and, folding her against his heart, he held her until the fever cooled and she could breathe again.

Then he moved away, started the engine and drove off, going back to the main road. He said nothing, and for a while she thought he was taking her back to his house, but then he headed for the town centre and the hospital, and she felt a wash of relief amidst the frustration.

He pulled up in the car park, turned off the engine and then sat in silence for a moment before turning to her. 'Frankie, you know where this is leading, don't you?' he murmured.

She reached out and took his hand. 'Yes, I know.'

His eyes searched hers by the dim glow of the lighting along the pavements. 'I don't want to rush into anything,' he told her. 'I don't think it's a good idea to mix work and home, but we seem to have done that since the first day.'

He looked away, his hand turning over in hers and caressing her fingers. 'I need you, Frankie. I haven't felt like this for years, if ever. I don't want to rush it, hurry things and spoil it. I also want you and Jane to get to know each other, because whatever happens we're a package deal.'

She slipped her hand out of his and touched his face. 'I know that, Robert. Don't worry. We'll take it as it comes. Just be honest with me—whatever you feel, tell me. Even if we end up going nowhere, let's have the truth between us.'

Their eyes locked for an age, then she leant over and dropped a gentle kiss on his lips. 'I'll see you in the morning,' she murmured, and, getting out of the car, she headed for the hospital entrance without a backward glance. At the door she turned and lifted a hand, and his lights flashed on and off and he started the engine and drove away.

She went back to her room, passing Gavin again on the way in.

'Is everything all right?' he asked her.

She smiled, unable to stop herself. 'Yes, of course.'

'I just wondered—he looked pretty mad with you.'

'No—actually he was mad with someone else,' she told him, but didn't add that it was him.

'Just thought I'd check—wouldn't want you to end up dead in a ditch somewhere without anybody caring,' he said with a laugh. 'I'll see you, Frankie. Take care.'

'I will.'

She let herself into her room and closed the door, then caught sight of herself in the mirror. Her hair was mussed and her lips looked—well, kissed. She laughed, and wondered fleetingly what Gavin must have thought. Then the smile faded as she remembered Robert's words.

'I need you, Frankie. I haven't felt like this for years, if ever. I don't want to rush it. . .' She smiled again. If the gear lever hadn't been in the way they would almost certainly have rushed all sorts of things. It was years since anyone had kissed her in a car. She'd almost forgotten how appallingly uncomfortable and how incredibly exciting it was.

Then she remembered the rest of his words. 'I also want you and Jane to get to know each other, because whatever happens we're a package deal.'

Well, she and Jane seemed to be getting on all right, but Jane wouldn't be part of a deal that just involved an affair, so maybe he had more in mind? Or maybe he was just up front with his daughter about his relationships.

Time would tell. Humming softly, she got ready for bed, climbed in with an orthopaedics textbook and wished it were Robert instead.

'We'll excise this length of bone from here to here, clean out all the rubbish and fill him full of antibiotics, put a drain in and then sit back and wait,' Robert told her as they stood in front of the light box and studied Jim Pate's X-rays.

'What about this bit here?' she asked, and as she reached up to point at the plate she brushed against him. The air all but crackled, but she tried her best to ignore it and concentrate. 'The bone looks a little dodgy on X-ray.'

Beside her she heard a quiet sigh, then Robert's head shifted slightly and he gave the plate his attention. 'Yes, you could be right. We'll see. The best thing to do is open him up, but we need to get the external fixators on before we start hacking him around. Right, are you ready?'

She gave a hollow laugh. 'As I'll ever be.'

He put his hand on her shoulder and squeezed gently. 'You'll do fine. If when we open him up I think it's too much for you I'll take over, so don't worry.'

'Your confidence in me doesn't tally with my own,' she said drily.

'You can always bottle out if you can't cope,' he said reasonably, but she chuckled.

'No way, Robert. I wouldn't give you the satisfaction.'

They went through into the operating room and he talked Frankie through the setting up of the external fixators, the frame outside his leg which would hold the limb rigid even though a chunk of bone was missing from the middle and it was technically unsupported. Once the fixators were on to his satisfaction, he told her to open the leg, and they were then able to see the hole in the bone and the damage done by years of chronic suppuration.

She freed and cut away the section of bone they were to remove, took out the lump of dead bone inside and cleaned the area as well as possible, then sewed a corrugated drainage strip in position to speed recovery and packed the wound. They couldn't close it, not with that level of infection, and once the wound was clean they would need to graft a new section of bone into the gap. In the meantime they would watch him closely.

As Frankie finished she was aware of a great sense of satisfaction and even pride in a job well done. As the patient was wheeled out to Recovery and she and Robert went through for coffee, stripping off their gloves and gowns as they went, she threw back her head and laughed.

'Why are you so damned happy?' Robert grumbled beside her.

'Because I did that well. It was difficult and challenging and you were right, I could do it, and I enjoyed it, and I feel really self-satisfied.'

His smile was wry. 'I'm so glad. All I feel is frustrated.'

Her eyes clashed with his and they exchanged a rueful grin. 'Me too,' she confessed softly. 'Last night was so long.'

'Don't,' he groaned. 'Here, have a coffee and go and sit over there and try and look ugly for a minute so I can get my breath back.'

She chuckled again, and he closed his eyes and sighed. 'Oh, Frankie, what am I going to do with you?' he asked quietly. 'You drive me crazy.'

'You could always do the obvious,' she suggested.

His eyes slowly opened and he stared at her, then sighed and shut them again. 'God, woman, you pick your moments,' he muttered.

Peter Graham stuck his head round the door. 'Your next patient's ready for you,' he said. 'You want me to knock her out?'

Robert glanced at him without interest, then sighed and stood up. 'Yes, please. We'll be through in a second. Come on, Dr Bradley; time's a-wasting and I want this day over with. I'm on a promise and I don't intend to let you forget it.'

With that look in his eyes? she thought. No chance.

Fate, however, was not on their side. As the morning drew on, so Robert began to look flushed and bright-eyed, and at one point he swayed alarmingly, then righted himself with a muttered apology and carried on.

He was operating on a child's forearm at the time, fixing the radius and ulna, which had both snapped following a fall from a swing onto his outstretched hand. He had pinned the ulna and was attempting to pin the radius when Frankie realised that he was far from well and about to collapse.

'Robert, do you want me to take over?' she asked.

He lifted his head and stared vacantly at her. 'Flu,' he mumbled, and swayed again.

Frankie sighed. She had never pinned a radius, but she had watched him do it and was pretty sure she knew how. She was also pretty sure that in his right mind he would have plated that particular break. 'Get him out, someone, and let him lie down somewhere,' she asked. 'I'll take him home in a while.'

He didn't protest, almost falling through the door and leaving Frankie encased in an expectant silence. She looked round. 'Pin or plate?' she asked the assembled company.

'Er—I think he would plate that, to be honest,' the scrub nurse told her.

'That's what I thought,' Frankie agreed. 'Suppose we finish this one together, eh, chaps?'

Half an hour later the little boy's operation was finished, the anaesthetic reversed and he was in Recovery.

Frankie stripped off her gloves and gown, dropped them in the bin and went to find Robert. He was stretched out in the rest room along three chairs, a dark flush on his cheekbones and black shadows under his eyes. His skin was scorching and dry to the touch and he was almost unaware of her.

With a shake of her head she went into the changing

room, showered and dressed and came back out. A male member of staff was just coming out of the changing room and, giving him Robert's locker key, she asked for all his things. Bundling them into a plastic bag but retaining the keys so that they could get into his house, she went back to find him.

He was sprawled just as she had left him, but he was shivering now and clearly getting worse.

'Come on, Robert, time to go home,' she told him, and he cranked open one eye and groaned.

'Headache,' he complained.

'I'm sure. You've got this nasty flu bug. Come on, I'll take you home now.' She put his coat on over his operating clothes, hoisted him up, tucked her head under his arm and straightened up. He sagged against her, and she had to enlist the help of a porter to get him into a wheelchair and down to the car park.

Once in the car she drove him quickly back to his house, opened the door and then had to coax, cajole and half carry him in.

The stairs almost defeated her, but she knew he needed to be safely tucked up in bed so she persevered, round the tight, curving staircase and up to the landing.

'Robert, where's your bedroom?' she asked him.

He mumbled something totally unintelligible, said, 'Sick,' and dived through a doorway. She followed him into the bathroom, held his head and then washed his face and gave him a glass of water to rinse with.

When he was a little steadier she managed to get him out onto the landing again and along to what she assumed was his bedroom.

'In here?' she asked, and he nodded slightly.

She yanked back the quilt, lowered him on to the mattress and then peeled off his wax jacket and theatre pyjamas. 'Such sartorial elegance, dear boy,' she teased him, and, leaving him the scant decency of his briefs, she tugged the quilt up over him, found a bowl and a couple of towels from downstairs and sat herself down at the foot of the bed with the phone.

Nick Davidson, the other orthopaedic firm's SR, was very obliging and agreed to cover the post-ops and any overnight problems. David Hunt, their SR, was doing the clinic that afternoon anyway.

Their cover arranged, Frankie settled down to sick-room duty.

'What time is it?'

Frankie opened her eyes and blinked. 'Six.'

'Morning or evening?'

'Evening. How are you?'

He struggled to a sitting position. 'Better. Hell, that was a vile little number.'

'It is. Short but sharp. You'll probably be fine tomorrow.'

He grunted and laid his head back with a sigh. 'Did you manage to finish the op?'

'Mmm—I plated the radius instead of pinning it.'

'Of course—you wouldn't be able to pin that radius because of the nature of the fracture.'

'Then it's a good job I took over from you, isn't it? Because you were struggling to pin it.'

His eyes widened. 'I was?'

Her smile was gentle. 'You were—but only till you nearly fell over.'

He shut his eyes and groaned. 'God, I felt ill. I thought I was just overheating because you were near me.'

She laughed, a little laugh that bubbled up and grew until he joined in weakly. 'Oh, Robert, do you really find me such a turn-on that your temperature goes up three degrees?'

He chuckled. 'Easily. I have to say I don't feel that

racked with passion now. I don't think God wants me to make love to you, Frankie.'

She gave a little spurt of laughter and reached for his hand, stroking it tenderly. 'I'm sure God is far too busy to worry about anything so trivial.'

'Trivial? I can assure you my feelings are far from trivial, Frankie.'

'In global terms. . .'

'Even so. I should think on the Richter scale—'

'Now I know you're exaggerating.'

They laughed softly, and then he coughed and pressed his hand to his chest.

'Sore?' she asked.

'Mmm. I could do with some painkillers.'

'I'll get you some. Where are they?'

'Bathroom cabinet.' He reached out and caught her hand, holding her near him for a moment. 'Thank you, Frankie. You're a life-saver.'

She smiled at him and pressed a kiss to his forehead. 'My pleasure. I had plans to spend this evening in your bedroom anyway.'

'Wicked hussy,' he murmured.

She would have liked to be, but she didn't think he could oblige if his life depended on it.

She settled instead for sharing a cup of tea with him after he had taken his painkillers, and then, satisfied that he would be all right, she went into Jane's bedroom, raided an oversize T-shirt from one of the drawers and tucked herself up in Jane's bed.

She left the door open so that she could hear if Robert needed her, but the only sound was the occasional soft snore as he slept.

With a rueful but contented smile she snuggled down under the quilt, turned out the bedside light and went to sleep. . .

*   *   *

'Rise and shine.'

She blinked open her eyes and stared around her, totally disorientated for a moment. Then her bleary eyes took in Robert, propped in the doorway in a short towelling dressing gown that did fascinating things to her blood pressure, looking pale but otherwise recovered and much too sexy for her peace of mind.

She struggled to a sitting position, tucked the quilt firmly under her armpits and shoved a hand through her tumbled hair. 'What time is it?' she asked huskily.

'Seven. I thought you'd gone home, but then I saw your car outside.'

'I didn't know how you'd be. You might have needed me in the night.'

Their eyes met and he gave a wry chuckle. 'Oh, I needed you all right, Frankie. I just wasn't up to doing anything about it.'

She blushed and looked away. With a heavy shadow on his jaw and that indecent dressing gown he was playing havoc with her sanity. Those legs! she thought, and dragged her eyes away from them. It didn't help. She could still see them out of the corner of her eye, the scatter of curls dark against the skin that lay taut over the long, well-muscled limbs.

'How would you like to get dressed?' she suggested a little unevenly.

'I was just going to say the same to you.'

She glanced up at him, the laughter in his eyes strangely at odds with the need that raged beside it.

'We ought to just get on with it,' she said abruptly.

'I quite agree, but I want to be at the hospital by eight and when I do make love to you, Frankie, I want longer than ten minutes to do it.'

And with that he was gone.

She fell back against the pillows with a ragged sigh. How on earth was she going to get through a weekend at Center Parcs with him? Jane was going to have her work cut out chaperoning them, she thought with a grim laugh, especially if they were already lovers by then, because one thing was for sure—it would take more than a few days to quench the fire that raged in them.

Fate, yet again, was not on their side. That day was busy, starting with a ward round to make sure that the child whose operation she had completed was doing well and hadn't come to any lasting harm as far as could be seen, and that Jim Pate was comfortable and the wound was draining as it ought.

Robert was feeling washed out and still less than a hundred per cent, so she shared the work with David Hunt and he went home to rest, having satisfied himself that the world hadn't come to an end because he'd taken an afternoon off.

Frankie covered the night, and, predictably, she thought, because she was on it was hectic.

A spate of road accidents on the ice brought in several people with fractures. Some were plastered and sent home, others admitted for observation in the A and E department.

Two came up to the ward for surgery the following day to reduce fractures, including one man with a badly shattered femur. Frankie put him on traction to pull the bones out into approximate alignment and relax the muscles holding the limb in contraction, and once she was happy that he was stable and substantially pain-free she went back down to A and E to see what was going on with the others.

The three in the observation ward on A and E were settling well so she returned to the ward to check on the two up there. Barry Long, the man with the shattered femur, showed signs of deterioration, possibly from internal injuries and possibly from heavy bleeding from the fracture site; although Frankie thought that the latter was the most likely she called the surgical reg on take just to be on the safe side.

The patient was already receiving a blood transfusion and she instructed the nurses to squeeze the blood in by hand, then had another look at him. A little while later Gavin Jones appeared, bleary-eyed but smiling.

'Hello, trouble,' he said with a grin. 'What's the problem?'

She chewed her lip. 'I'm not sure. RTA victim. He's got a badly shattered thigh—lots of soft tissue damage, but the pulse in his foot is good and the lower leg is reasonably well. His blood pressure's dropping, though, and he's going into shock. He's not looking too good, I'm afraid. I think it's the femur, but I didn't want to overlook the possiblity of abdominal haemorrhage.'

'Was he driving?'

'I think so.'

'So it could be steering-wheel damage. I think we may need to stick a needle in his abdomen and see if there's any blood there, but you know you can lose up to half the blood volume with a fractured femur if it's bad enough. Let's have a look at him.'

They went to his bedside, and Gavin quickly and gently palpated his abdomen then shook his head. 'It's quite soft. Let's have a look at this femur.' He turned back the bedclothes further and caught his lip between his teeth. 'That looks a very bad injury, Frankie. I think you ought to go in and find that leak. It's not the femoral artery but it might well be the femoral vein. I think you need to call Ryder out.'

She looked at the limb and realised how much it had swollen since she had called Gavin. 'I'll do it now, and alert Theatre and get him prepped up. We'll need to shave the leg.' She turned to the staff nurse beside her. 'Could you prepare him for Theatre and send him straight up? I'll get Mr Ryder.'

Gavin came with her to the nursing station, waited while she made the call and then offered his help. 'Do you want me to come in with you until he arrives? Just for moral support?'

She shook her head. 'I'll be OK, Gavin, thanks. I'm sorry I got you up for nothing.'

'Don't worry about it. Rather you than me with that leg; it looks a mess.'

It was, but fortunately Robert arrived with the patient and was scrubbed and beside her just as she was preparing to go in.

'I'll do it,' he said tersely, and with a swift stroke of the scalpel he opened the skin. Blood immediately started to pour from the wound. 'Hell's teeth,' he muttered. 'How is he?'

'Stable—just,' the anaesthetist replied.

'Keep bagging that blood in, please. Can somebody hoover this mess up?' he snapped, and, as the scrub nurse sucked out the wound, without wasting time on finesse he cut down to the vein, grabbed it in his fingers and squashed it flat. 'Can we have forceps on here, please?' he said.

The scrub nurse was there already, clamping off the vein before the sentence was finished. Frankie, largely redundant, watched him work to suture the torn section of vein and remove some of the shattered bits of bone that would never be of any use, then he set to work to pin and plate the fragmented bone.

'Normally I'd pull a bone like this out by traction and let it heal naturally to minimise any further trauma,' he told her, 'but as we're in we may as well fix it. It's going to be a pretty patchy job anyway; it's not a nice fracture.'

Frankie thought that the understatement of the century. The muscles were lacerated by the bone ends, the nerves were stretched and although probably not permanently damaged were certainly challenged, and the bone was going to heal at least a centimetre shorter because of the shattered ends.

Robert finally closed the wounds, stretched and turned to the anaesthetist.

'He's all yours. Thanks. How is he now?'

'Better. Stabilising well.'

Robert nodded, tugged off his mask and walked out, followed closely by Frankie. 'I'm sorry I called you,' she began, but he shook his head.

'That was very nasty. I wouldn't expect you to handle that. I'm glad you called me when you did, otherwise we could have lost him. The trauma had caused such a big rip in the muscles that there was a huge hole there to fill with blood. He was lucky to get away with it.' He gave a wry chuckle. 'I expect in two weeks he'll be complaining that it's shorter than the other one and threatening to sue us.'

She grinned. 'I'm glad you did the op, then.'

'Humph. Cheeky minx. Fancy a coffee?'

She declined. 'I ought to go and check the others.'

'Others?'

'Oh, yes,' she told him. 'We've had three RTAs in—the place has been like Piccadilly.'

'And you kept all the fun to yourself?'

'Not quite all,' she said with a grin. 'You got the best bit, and I got Gavin up to look at our friend here because I wondered if it was an abdominal bleed. Oh, and I signed the consent form for Barry Long, by the way, with the night sister, so I hope he makes it.'

'He'll live—just long enough to sue.'

She chewed her lip. 'Do you think so?'

He laughed. 'No. Don't worry, he'll be grateful. I'll

make sure he knows how close he came, and that he had my personal attention.'

'He'll be very impressed,' Frankie said with wide eyes.

'Are you being sarcastic, madam?'

'Me?' She grinned. 'Of course not. Since you're here, do you want to cast your expert eye over the others?'

He returned the grin. 'I might as well, as you've got me up—see how much of a hash you've made of the rest of them.'

'Damn cheek.'

'Come on. I'll give you the name and address of my solicitor if you're very nice to me and give me some of that cake.'

'It's finished, remember? And Jane and I didn't get round to baking another one at the weekend.'

'Good.' He shot her a crooked grin. 'I don't think you'd be safe alone with me in that cosy little room of yours, somehow.'

And, judging by the look in his eyes, she had to agree with him. . .

CHAPTER SEVEN

FRIDAY arrived before Frankie had time to blink. The
ward was very busy with the emergency admissions,
and although their femur patient Barry Long had
settled well there was a constant flow of new patients
who needed her attention.

By Friday afternoon she was tired, crabby and ready
to get right away from it all. The warm salt pool and
crisp night air of Elvedon Forest called to her, and she
could hardly wait to get to their destination and dive
in head first.

Robert, on the other hand, was also tired and crabby
but obviously not looking forward to the weekend
at all.

'I can't imagine why I let you talk me into it,' he
grumbled at lunchtime. 'It's the last thing I need. I
should be decorating or doing the garden or
something.'

Frankie laughed. 'Rubbish. The house is fine, the
garden's too wet to do anything with and you need to
have some fun.'

He glowered morosely at her. 'It'll be like an up-
market holiday camp,' he grumbled. 'Rise and shine
and jolly hockey sticks—revolting.'

'Rubbish,' she said again. 'Robert, you'll love it. It's
beautiful. You can cycle through the woods—'

'I haven't ridden a bike for nearly twenty years.'

'It'll do you good. And if you're very well behaved
and pretend to be having fun I'll give you a massage.'

He gave a derisive snort. 'Jane'll be there.'

'So you'll have to behave. That'll do you good too.'

'I've done nothing but behave for years. I think I'm ready to break out.'

She regarded him thoughtfully. 'How many years, just as a matter of interest?'

He gave a short huff of laughter. 'Since I last had an affair? About five.'

Her eyes widened. 'Five years?' she all but squeaked.

He shrugged. 'There didn't seem to be anyone worth having a relationship with, and, to be honest, Jackie's behaviour has put me right off the thought of casual sex, if I ever found it appealing.'

And yet he was definitely ready to start an affair with her. Did that mean, in his words, that she was someone 'worth having a relationship with'? Suddenly that relationship seemed to take on much more significance, and Frankie looked at him with new eyes. Was he really that serious about her? He hadn't mentioned love, but then nor had she. Perhaps it was time to talk about it, and perhaps this weekend would be a good starting point.

She felt suddenly nervous, as if it was almost a test and as if her trial period was now expanded to include her suitability as a wife and mother, not just a colleague.

Would she pass?

Dear God, she hoped so. . .

'Can we swim now? Please, Dad, I want to find the pool. . .'

Despite the apparent sophistication of her thirteen years, Jane's eyes were wide with excitement, but Robert was concerned with practicalities and cut her off with a raised hand. 'In a minute. Let's just get sorted out in here first. We need food, we need bikes—' he shot Frankie a scathing look which she countered with a grin '—and we need to sort out who's having which room.'

'I'm having this one,' Jane said promptly, disappearing through a doorway with her suitcase. 'I'm getting out of this uniform and then can we *please* have a swim?'

Robert looked at Frankie, and then at the other two bedroom doors, side by side in the other corner of the room, and raised one eyebrow.

'No,' she said quietly but clearly. 'Not with Jane here.'

His mouth quirked. 'It was just a thought. If I sleepwalk—'

'You'll get bashed on the head. Right, which one are you having? You're bigger than me. Let's look.'

She poked her head round the doors and chose the smallest room. 'This one'll do me. OK?'

He shook his head. 'Frankie, I don't care. I won't sleep anyway, not with you so close.'

She laughed softly. 'Of course you will. You'll be shattered from all the exercise. Come.' She seized him by the hand and dragged him over to the patio doors. There was a lake stretched out in front of them, and some intrepid enthusiast was windsurfing in a wetsuit, skimming over the water towards them.

'How do you fancy having a go at that?'

He looked at her as if she'd grown two heads. 'In January?'

She shrugged. 'OK. How about a pedalo? We could stay dry then.'

'If it doesn't rain.'

She tutted and was about to take him to task when a slight movement caught her eye. She smiled involuntarily. 'Oh, look—by the edge of the patio.'

'Squirrels. I've got them in my garden.'

'Well, I haven't,' she retorted, and turned to face him. 'Robert, you are going to enjoy yourself,' she said firmly. 'Now go and change out of that suit, put on something casual, find your swimming gear and let's go and get the bikes and get to it.'

'But we need to sort the food out first.'

'No, we don't. We can eat out, and the supermarket stays open late. Come on,' she coaxed. 'For Jane's sake if nothing else, please at least *try* to enjoy it.'

With a sigh he picked up his case, disappeared into his room and shut the door firmly. With a shrug Frankie took her things through to her own room, unpacked a few essentials and changed into leggings and a loose sweatshirt top with her swimming things underneath, then went to find Jane.

She was sitting on the bed in a welter of new clothes, trying to choose what to wear. She looked at Frankie, selected something similar and shed her uniform into a pile on the floor.

'You could do with putting that away carefully, because you'll need it on Sunday and we can't wash it here,' Frankie pointed out.

She scraped it up with a good-natured grumble, folded it more or less neatly and tugged on her new clothes. 'Right, can we swim—? Hey, Dad, *jeans*?'

Frankie spun round and stared. My God, he looked *delectable*. He was gorgeous enough in formal clothes. In soft old bottom-hugging jeans he was just the absolute business. She gave a low, sexy whistle and he flushed and tried to look repressive, but her chuckle came out anyway.

'What's the matter? Can't you take a compliment?'

'Frankie, behave,' he growled, 'or I'll go and change.'

'Don't do that; they look really good.'

He arched a brow in disbelief but she could see that

he was pleased. 'They're ancient,' he told her. 'I found them amongst my gardening clothes. I've never worn them for gardening; they're too darned tight.'

Frankie had noticed. 'They suit you,' she said thoughtfully. 'Sort of halve your age, somehow.'

She ducked the rolled-up towel and came up laughing.

'He hates being teased,' Jane told her sagely. 'He gets a real grump on sometimes.'

Frankie grinned. 'I had noticed. OK, come on, let's get at it.'

Two hours later they were still in the pool. Jane had almost worn out the seat of her costume coming down the wild-water rapids, and they had been swept round an island in an amazingly powerful current, tried the cold plunge outside by the top of the rapids and voted it a masochist's dream come true, and ended up in the salt pool, swimming outside in a fine misting rain that finally turned to sleet.

Frankie, revelling in the contrast between icy rain and steaming water, turned her face up to the sky and laughed in sheer delight. Robert was beside her, just visible in the thick fog that hung over the surface of the water, and as their legs tangled she slipped one hand round the back of his neck and brushed her lips over his.

'Are you OK?' she asked.

'Yes—you were right, it's wonderful,' he said softly.

'There's no phone,' she told him.

'And no decorating or gardening.'

'Just having fun.'

'It seems so decadent.'

His leg slid up hers and down again, sending tingles down her spine.

'I think you need the cold plunge,' she told him with a knowing smile.

'I think you're right, but I'm damned if I'm going in it,' he replied, and under cover of the water his hand slid up and cupped her breast. 'God, Frankie, you are beautiful,' he murmured, suddenly serious, and she was on the point of kissing him again when Jane appeared out of the fog.

'Are you two all right?' she asked, a little frown wrinkling her brow. 'Only you look ever so serious.'

Frankie smiled at her reassuringly. 'We're fine. Your father just confessed he's having fun. It's a serious business for him; he's not used to it.'

She should have seen it coming but she didn't. Robert's arm arced over her, his hand cupped her icy head and she was dunked under the hot water. She swam away, hair streaming out behind her, and came up out of sight, laughing. He followed her, treading water a few feet away.

'JJ and I are going down the rapids again.'

'Fine. I'll be here,' she told them. 'Have fun.'

She floated quietly for a while, dipping under the hot water every now and again when the icy drizzle became too much, thinking about her relationship with Jane, and then after a while when the cold got to her she went back inside under the plastic strips across the entrance and sat on the steps.

Robert appeared at her side. 'She's just having one more go on the rapids and then I said we ought to change and get some shopping.'

'Where are we eating tonight?' she asked.

'In, if we can find anything easy. I'm shattered, Frankie; I could do with sitting down and putting my feet up.'

It sounded perfect. 'Me too,' she told him. 'I'll cook, shall I? I believe it's my turn.'

'Will we survive?' he teased.

'You survived the cake.'

His eyes lit up. 'So I did. Maybe this meal won't be so dire after all.'

'Dire? I'll give you dire—' She shoved, and he sprawled full length in the water, turning round to grab her ankle just as Jane arrived.

'Children, children,' she scolded. 'Come on, then, I'm starving.'

They had a huge deep-pan pizza with masses of mushrooms and tomatoes and peppers on it, and a crunchy green salad and lots of really buttery garlic bread, then for pudding a frozen chocolate gateau which they cut into chunks and then had to wait for while they washed up. Even so it was still frozen, but they didn't care. They collapsed in front of the television with it, feet up on the table, and within moments of finishing his gateau Robert's eyes had drooped shut.

'It's his age,' Jane informed Frankie confidentially, nibbling the gooey topping. 'They start dropping off all the time, you know.'

'It couldn't be anything to do with working hard or having had flu this week, I don't suppose?' he mumbled sleepily from the corner.

Frankie and Jane both giggled, and he cranked one eye open. 'Are you girls picking on me?' he complained.

'Of course not—go back to sleep,' Jane told him fondly.

They watched a video, and then finally even Jane's eyelids started to droop. 'I'm going to bed,' she said with a little smile. 'I'll see you tomorrow.'

She flitted in and out to the bathroom, then as her door closed for the last time Robert's eyes opened.

'Has she gone now?'

'I think so. Why?'

'Because,' he said softly, 'I could do with a cuddle.'

'Is that all?' she teased, her voice barely a whisper.

'No, but it's the nearest I'll get.'

She slid her hand along the sofa and linked her fingers with his. 'Closer,' he murmured, and so she wriggled along until her head was on his shoulder and his arm was round her, and hoped Jane wouldn't come out again.

'I want to make love to you,' he whispered.

'I know,' she whispered back, 'but you can't.'

'I know, but I want to.'

'I want you to too. We need distracting—tell me about your house,' she said.

'My house?' There was a catch of surprised laughter in his voice.

'Mmm—how long you've lived there, what it was like when you moved in—you know, all that sort of thing.'

He chuckled softly. 'You really want to know?'

'Mmm.'

'Well, it was a wreck when I first saw it,' he told her. 'The roof was dodgy, the front wall needed stripping right back to the timber frame and replastering, the interior was ghastly—it was a mess.

'The oak screen in the drawing room and hall—originally called the screen passage—was painted with bright blue gloss, the beams were all gloss of various colours, the floors were uneven and some of the bricks were up—it was awful. I had to have it gutted, sandblasted back to the oak and all the floors relaid.'

'So why did you buy it?' she asked him in amazement. 'I mean, you must have been busy at work—when was this? Two years ago?'

He nodded. 'When I got the consultancy. It was a fresh start, away from London and Jackie, somewhere I could give Jane real holidays in the country when she came up to stay with me. That was why I looked at it. I bought it, in spite of the terrible condition it was in, because I fell in love with the name.'

'Freedom Farm?'

His mouth tipped in a wry smile. 'I thought it would mean a whole new era. Instead Jackie followed me up here and imposed herself on me, saying she thought we ought to have another chance. It turned out she'd had a tiff with a boyfriend and he wouldn't move out.

'I told her she could have the guest room for a week, no more, and went down to London and turfed the sponger out. In that time she spent every evening in the pub flirting with the locals and complaining about the state of my place, and by the end of the week she was more than ready to go. I don't think any of the locals would play her games, although I gather she tried.'

He laughed without humour. 'She still comes up every now and again for the weekend, goes down to the pub and has a couple of gins and then expects me to fetch her.'

'Why do you tolerate it?' Frankie asked in amazement.

'For Jane,' he said simply, and that said it all. It was why he did everything, she realised—to give Jane a future, to give her a home with him now, to be her continuity in the crazy world her mother lived in. 'She should have been with me years ago,' he murmured, almost to himself. 'I've let her down. It's my fault she's alive. The least I could do was make sure that her life was safe and decent.'

Frankie laid her hand over his heart and listened with her body to the steady beat. 'I don't think you've let her down at all,' she told him gently. 'I think she's a lovely girl and I think you should be very proud of her. She's your daughter, not Jackie's. There isn't a flighty bone in her body; she's just like you. She's serious, conscientious—she loves you, Robert. I know she teases you, but it's because she feels safe. Cherished. I used to feel like that.'

Frankie felt a lump in her throat and swallowed it, and his arm tightened round her fractionally. 'What happened?' he asked quietly. 'You never talk about your family.'

She lifted a shoulder. 'They died. My mother had cancer and my father couldn't face life without her. He died at the wheel of his car. The verdict was accidental death, but I think he killed himself. He was sober, the road conditions were good and they found nothing wrong with the car. Mind you, the evidence could have been destroyed; he hit a bridge support at about eighty miles an hour.

'I was eighteen; my brother Jeff was twenty-two. He'd left university, got a job in London and was struggling to pay the mortgage on a new house. I got into medical school in London, moved in with him and gave him all I could spare of my grant, and in my free time I helped him do up the house. I lived there throughout my training, and then when I got a job too far away to commute I used to go back at the weekends and for holidays.

'Then he met Sue, and I began to feel rather *de trop*. They got married in September, and so I thought it might be time to move on, find another job out of London and get right away, give them some space. I'd like to buy a little place of my own, but I couldn't afford to in London so I thought I'd have a fresh start out here.' She looked up into his eyes. 'If I'm going to have a job, that is.'

His eyes softened. 'Of course you've got a job. You've got a long way to go before you're a consultant, but you're only twenty-eight, and you've got the potential to be an extremely gifted surgeon. Actually I'm beginning to realise how lucky I was to get you—in every way.'

His mouth drifted down towards her, its touch feather-light, and with a tiny sigh she snuggled closer and deepened the kiss.

'Oh, Frankie, I need you,' he murmured.

Her body melted at the soft, husky words, but there was something, someone—

She sighed and levered herself away, dragging her hands through her hair and sighing shakily. 'I need you too, but not now—not here, with Jane in her room.'

He gave a little huff of humourless laughter. 'I hadn't forgotten her, sweetheart. I just haven't got the self-control to keep right away from you.'

'Perhaps we should remove ourselves from temptation and go to our separate beds?' she suggested.

'Why don't we just lie here and watch a video and try and keep our hands to ourselves?'

'Do you think we can?'

He laughed. 'Probably not. Here, let's rearrange ourselves.'

The seating was in a continuous L-shape, and he lay one way with his back propped in the corner and patted the other side. Frankie lay down at right angles, so that her head was pillowed on his lap and her cheek lay against the soft, worn denim of his jeans.

'You look really good in these,' she told him, stroking the fabric absently.

'Hell, Frankie,' he muttered, and shifted under her, uncomfortably aroused.

'You wanted to lie here and push your luck,' she reminded him mischievously.

'Hmm. Watch the film.'

'I've seen it.'

'So've I.'

'Robert, I'm going to bed before I rip your clothes off.'

She stood up and looked down at him, sexy and rumpled, his eyes smoky with desire, and wondered how they were going to make it to Sunday night.

As sure as eggs were eggs, they wouldn't last a minute longer. . .

The phone was ringing as they stepped over the threshold. Rolling his eyes, Robert reached for it. 'Hello, Ryder here.'

There was a pause, then he said, 'When? Oh, hell.' He closed his eyes and sighed. 'I'll be right with you, Nick. Thanks.'

Frankie met his eyes. 'Trouble?'

'That was Nick Davidson. Barry Long—the guy with the shattered femur—has got a massive pulmonary embolus and they've moved him to ITU. He's looking pretty grim, apparently. I ought to go in.'

'Will you be long?'

His eyes met hers, hungry and frustrated. 'I don't know. I hope not, but I probably will be. Do you want me to give you a lift back?'

He was standing on the other side of the hall, too far away to touch, and suddenly she felt desperately unsure. 'Do you want me to go?' she asked at last.

'God, no. Frankie, you know I don't.'

'Then I'll stay,' she said simply.

He hugged her briefly, ran upstairs to change out of his jeans and ran back down. 'I'll ring if I'm held up,' he promised, and seconds later he gunned the engine and shot down the drive.

The house seemed curiously empty without him, but it was a gentle emptiness, not a cold and inhospitable feeling but more one of expectation. Perhaps that was just her, she thought with a nervous laugh.

She decided to light the fire in the sitting room, then, looking through the CDs, she found the original of the love album that had nearly caused Robert to crash the car the previous week. She put it on, made a cup of tea and curled up with it in his chair, letting the music move her.

She loved his chair. If she turned her head she could sometimes catch the faintest hint of his aftershave. He only wore it occasionally, but he had worn it this weekend, and it and the music were very evocative. She felt closer to him somehow, as if he was less of a stranger.

In truth he was a bit of a stranger. What did she really know about him, the real Robert Ryder? He had revealed a little of his history, but almost nothing of his heart. Had she been any more open? She didn't think so. Perhaps tonight—

The phone rang, shattering the silence. She answered it cautiously, but it was Robert.

'We've lost him,' he said shortly, and she could hear the frustration in his voice. 'I'm just going to spend some time with his relatives and then I'll be back. Are you all right?'

'Yes. I'm sorry about Barry.'

'So am I. I'll see you soon.'

There was a click, and then the dialling tone. She put down the receiver and thought about the man with the shattered femur who had nearly bled to death five days before, and wondered why they thought they could play God. Had they left him he would have died then and been spared the suffering of the past few days.

And if they had they would have spent the rest of their lives wondering if they couldn't have done something to save him.

Medicine, she decided, was a very strange way of life. She settled down to wait for Robert.

His relatives were devastated. How had it happened? How could something so unrelated to his leg have killed him? Did he have chest injuries? They were clots. Where from? The leg—so not unrelated? Whose fault was it, then? Theirs? They had bought him the car he had been driving—

'It's nobody's fault,' Robert said gently. 'Sometimes these things just happen. The road conditions were appalling, apparently. His injury was very severe. The operation was necessary to save his life, and nothing could have been done to anticipate this next crisis.'

'What about anticoagulants?' his sister wanted to know. 'You put him on them today—why not before?'

'Because he had a great deal of bleeding into the muscles. With anticoagulant therapy the bleeding might not have stopped, and he could have died of that.'

'Heads you win, tails I lose,' his father muttered. 'Somebody's law, isn't it? Oh, God, what have we done?' His face crumpled and he buried it in his hands, his shoulders heaving.

His daughter ran to comfort him, crying on his shoulder and making soothing noises through her tears.

Only the mother stood there in silence, saying nothing. Then Robert noticed her lips moving, as if in prayer. 'I'm very sorry, Mrs Long,' he said quietly. 'I just wish there'd been more we could have done.'

'The Lord moves in mysterious ways,' she said in a dead voice. 'No doubt one day there'll be some sense to be made of it. Come on, Matthew, Helen. Let's go home.'

He watched them go, then filled in the report that would close the file and left the hospital.

Frankie was waiting for him at the house. She would expect him to be simmering with lust as he had been for the past week or more, but instead he just felt empty inside.

Empty and curiously scared. Would he let her down? God, it had been so long he wasn't sure he still knew what to do. He wasn't very hot on courtship, and with that young man's death looming so large in his mind it wasn't the best time.

He would try, though. Dear God, he would try, because she deserved the best he could give her and more. She was wonderful—lively, funny, full of that amazing energy that made him feel about a hundred in the shade, and yet so gentle and giving, so kind, so loving.

Suddenly he could hardly wait to get home to her— not to make love to her, but just to hold her and be held, to share the sorrow of their failure and talk about what had gone wrong.

And then, when the dust had settled and he was at peace again, he would love her as she deserved to be loved. . .

Frankie heard the car on the drive and opened the door to him as he approached, the doorkey in his hand.

'Hi,' she said softly. 'Need a hug?'

'How did you know?' he sighed, and, dropping his keys on the settle, he walked into her open arms. She hugged him gently, feeling the tension inside him giving way to the curious exhaustion of mind that failure left in its wake.

'Come and have a drink and tell me all about it,' she offered, and with a quick squeeze he let her go and followed her through into the sitting room.

'You lit the fire,' he said in surprise.

'I thought you'd need cheering up. Port?'

'Mmm. Frankie, you're a life-saver.' He dropped into his chair, kicked off his shoes and sighed heavily.

She poured him a hefty measure of his birthday port and took it over to him, then sat in the other chair across from him and waited for him to talk. He would, she knew, just as soon as he was ready.

'His mother and father and sister were all there,' he said finally. 'They watched a young man die and couldn't understand it, and I didn't have the words to explain it to them.' He shook his head. 'I just wish I could find an easy way to say "I'm sorry, your loved one's dead". There just isn't one, is there? And when they're young, as he was—ah, hell, it's just so unfair.'

He rambled on for a while, cursing fate, running over the treatment and debating the problems, then finally he ran out of steam and fell silent.

Frankie watched him. What he needed was loving, someone holding him and taking him away from reality to a magic place where pain didn't exist. She had been playing Jane's love album on the CD player, and she rose now and put it on again, just softly in the background, then went over to him, holding out her hand.

'Dance with me,' she murmured.

He hesitated for a second, then slowly stood, put the glass down and took her in his arms.

Her head fitted on his shoulder as if they were made for each other, she thought, and, locking her hands behind his back, she swayed with him to the pulsing, tender beat.

At first he was stiff, a little reluctant, but then he relaxed against her, holding her closer, his lips nuzzling her neck as they moved softly to the music.

Then he turned his head a little more and his lips found hers with a ragged sigh. The music forgotten, they stood almost motionless in the room as the kiss stretched on and on, gentle and undemanding, a tender question and a sweet reply.

His hand found hers and without words he led her up to his room and drew her into his arms again, resting his head against hers and letting out a shaky breath.

'Frankie, I don't know what this is going to be like,' he muttered. 'All I know is I want you more than I've ever wanted anything or anyone, but I don't think I'm going to be able to hold on—'

'Shh.' She covered his mouth with her hand, then, stepping back, she eased her leggings and bikini briefs down in one, then straightened up and stripped the sweatshirt over her head so that she stood naked before him.

'Oh, God, Frankie,' he breathed, and she could see the need etched in his face.

She moved closer, unbuttoning his shirt and sliding it down over his shoulders, leaving it trapping his wrists as she drew her hands slowly down over his chest, testing the texture of the curls, especially that little one at his throat that tormented her so. . .

'Frankie, please,' he groaned, and she took pity on him and released his hands; then, unbuckling his belt and slipping the hook on his trousers, she slid the zip down and let them fall.

He kicked them aside, and she knelt at his feet and took his socks off one by one. His legs drew her, and she ran her hands up them, savouring the tightly corded muscles that jumped beneath her hands, the wiry hair, and under it the satin-smooth skin, so warm against her palms.

Then she hooked her fingers in the top of his briefs and eased them down. She heard his sharp intake of breath and sat back on her heels, looking up at him.

He was perfect—lean, hard, a powerful man in his prime—and she loved him.

He reached for her, lifting her to her feet, then drew her into his arms again, swaying softly to the rhythm of the love song still playing quietly downstairs.

His body felt so good, so right against hers that Frankie could have wept. She felt the soft chafing of his hair against her aching breasts, the nudge of his arousal against her thighs, and beneath her hands his body trembled slightly. Desire tugged at her, and her hands rested on his hips as she swayed gently against him.

'You're so beautiful,' he whispered unevenly. 'I'm almost afraid to touch you.'

'Don't be,' she murmured. 'I'm all yours. Please touch me; I want you to.'

'God, Frankie, I need you,' he said rawly, and, easing away from him, she turned back the quilt and slipped between the icy sheets.

'Come. . .'

'I will—and probably far too soon, I'm afraid,' he said with a trace of humour as he slid in beside her.

She touched his beloved face. 'Don't be afraid. I love you, Robert.'

For a moment he was motionless, then, with a shattered groan, he gathered her in his arms and held her close. 'Oh, Frankie,' he breathed, and then he was moving over her, into her, his body hers at last and hers his, until she forgot where she ended and he began.

Then he moved, and the burning, blazing need exploded in her and she cried out, clinging to him in the chaos of her emotions. Seconds later his body arched against her and a deep cry was torn from his throat as the fire caught him too.

As the flaming, aching need burned itself out his head fell against her shoulder and his lips found the damp skin of her throat, just over the hammering pulse that measured her love for him.

'Are you all right?' he murmured at last.

'Mmm. Wonderful. You?'

'Oh, Frankie.' He gave a shaky laugh. 'That was—I don't know where to start. I'm not very good with words.'

'Just tell me what you feel.'

He was silent for a moment, then he said, very softly, 'Cherished. No one's ever told me before that they love me—certainly not my wife. Only Jane, and that's different.' He let his breath out on a gusty sigh. 'I'm sorry. I just feel so—'

He broke off, resting his head against her shoulder, and with infinite care she wrapped her arms around him and held him close against her heart. He was thirty-five and no one had told him they loved him? Dear God. . . She felt the hot, salty tears track down her temples and run into her hair, and then she felt another tear, this one his, run down over her shoulder.

After a moment he lifted his head and kissed her very softly on the mouth. 'I'm sorry. It's been a grim evening; I feel raw inside. You just touched a nerve.'

'I know. Don't worry; I understand. Sometimes it's all too much.'

'I can't stop thinking about Barry. He was so young to die, and it was so needless.'

She rubbed her hands gently down his back. 'It was nobody's fault,' she reminded him.

'They bought him the car.'

'Then they'll have to deal with that, but he wasn't a child. We can't play God to that extent. Right from childhood we have to make judgements and decisions about our own lives. Nobody can make them for us, or live our lives their way. Barry Long lived his way, and his luck ran out. It can be regretted, but no one should feel guilty.'

He sighed. 'I know you're right. I still feel sad, though.'

'You should. That's part of what I love about you.'

'Oh, Frankie.' He kissed her tenderly. 'I want to tell you that I love you, but I can't be sure if it's true or just what I want to feel.'

'You'll find out in time,' she murmured gently. 'Just give the feelings room; let them grow.'

His lips found hers again. 'Frankie?' he mumbled, nibbling gently. 'Can we try that again, but slowly this time?'

She smiled, and wound her arms round his neck. 'That sounds delightful. Where would you like to start?'

'Here?' His lips nibbled her ear.

'Hmm—maybe. . .'

'Or here?' He moved down over her throat.

'Warmer,' she murmured.

'Or here, perhaps?' His mouth closed over one aching, tender nipple and she gasped.

'Here, definitely,' he said with a little chuckle, and sucked deeply.

Frankie said nothing. For almost the first time in her life she was speechless. . .

CHAPTER EIGHT

IF FRANKIE thought her new intimacy with Robert would make any difference at work she was mistaken. If anything he pushed her harder, giving her more responsibility and spending less time working by her side.

She found herself having to make decisions about treatment, and although he was always ready to listen he made her tell him what should be done and why.

Sometimes she was way off beam, but more usually she was right, and her confidence in herself increased in leaps and bounds.

Darren Hawkes, the cyclist with the skin grafts, was recovering well despite her reservations, and although the skin looked very raw and tender at first Robert assured her it was a good result and would heal beautifully in time. Darren was discharged to Outpatients, and would continue to be seen for some time to assess the progress and function of his still extremely tender ankle.

Jim Pate, her osteomyelitis patient, became her sole responsibility and she found his slow but steady progress very rewarding. Two weeks after his operation the infection was clear in his wound and they were able to start the process of rebuilding his leg.

It was decided to take bone from both sides of his pelvis and graft it into the space left by the excision of the dead bone. If all went well his leg would end up scarred but functional, and relatively pain-free given time.

'So who's doing it?' she asked Robert.

'You.'

'Me?' she squeaked. 'I've never done a bone graft.'

He grinned. 'Well, it's time to expand your education, then.'

'Robert, you will be there, won't you?'

'Of course I will. Don't worry, Frankie, you'll be fine.'

She was, too, but it was still a comfort having him there.

'See? You didn't need me at all,' he said afterwards.

'I wouldn't say that,' she murmured.

He gave a strangled laugh. 'Hell, Frankie, don't. What are you doing tonight?'

She gave a slow smile. 'I can't imagine.'

He tapped her on the bottom. 'Go and check your patient. I'll see you later.'

Jim Pate was back on the ward by the time she got there after their list. He was awake but drowsy, and gave her a sleepy smile.

'Have I died or is it Dr Bradley?' he mumbled.

'You've died. How do you feel?'

'Sore but OK.'

She grinned. 'Good. That means I haven't destroyed the nerves. I suppose you're going to be demanding and want some painkillers next.'

He gave a tiny huff of laughter. 'What ever gave you that idea?'

She checked the chart, wrote him up for pethidine then went and found the ward sister.

'Mary, have we got a pethidine pump available? Jim Pate's suffering a bit.'

'No, I'm sorry, Frankie, they're all in use. He'll have to have it the traditional way. Do you want him to have some now?'

She nodded. 'I think so. He's in quite a bit of pain,

even though he's being brave. Do you want me to do it?'

'Could you? We're a bit pushed.'

She gave him the injection, assured him that he would soon feel the benefit and then went down to A and E in answer to her bleeper.

By the evening she was tired, her feet ached and she was ready for bed.

So was Robert. 'How about a nice hot bath and a rub down with a consultant?' he suggested once they were back at his house.

She smiled. 'Sounds wonderful. Which consultant did you have in mind? Oliver Henderson? Jack Lawrence? Ross Hamilton's rather good-looking.'

'He's too old for you,' Robert growled.

'Oh, I don't know. A bit of finesse, you know.'

Robert went suddenly still. 'I know I'm not the best lover. . .'

Frankie was appalled. 'Robert, what are you talking about? I was joking!'

'Yes, well, many a true word and all that.'

'Robert, look at me.' She took his face in her hands and turned him towards her. 'I love you,' she said clearly. 'Do you understand what I'm saying? What it means to me? What *you* mean to me?'

'So, you can forgive my clumsiness—'

'Robert, you are not clumsy!'

'Frankie, forget it.'

'No. Come with me.'

She grabbed him by the hand and towed him up the stairs into the bathroom. Then she turned on the taps, ran the bath and took off all their clothes.

'Get in,' she ordered.

He stared at her for a moment, then with a sigh he climbed into the big old claw-footed tub and sat down at the tap end.

'Other way.'

He moved, and she climbed in and sat between his knees, leaning back against his chest with a sigh of contentment. She handed him the soap. 'Wash me,' she said.

'Frankie—'

'Please?'

He started clinically enough, as if he were washing a child, but soon his movements changed, his hands lingering, smoothing, drawing circles of lather on her skin and playing hell with her blood pressure.

Finally, unable to bear it any longer, she took the soap off him, turned round and faced him.

'Kneel up,' she ordered gently.

They knelt face to face while she washed him with meticulous attention to detail, leaving no part of him untouched.

By the time she'd finished he was trembling all over and his eyes were on fire.

She took a sponge and rinsed him down, inch by inch, and then at last she stood up and stepped out, holding out her hand. 'Shall we go to bed?'

'No, we shan't,' he muttered. 'I can't walk that far. Come here.'

There was a chair in the bathroom which he used as a clothes-horse and, throwing their things off it, he sat down and drew her onto his lap.

It was incredible. His mouth was on a level with her breasts and he nuzzled them while he gently towelled her dry; then, lifting her, he settled her over his hips and entered her with one long, slow thrust.

Her breath caught in her throat and, resting her hands on his shoulders to steady herself, she moved slowly against him.

He shuddered. 'Frankie, I'm not going to last if you do that,' he groaned.

'Good. Nor am I.' She rocked against him, crying out at the sensation, and, cupping her bottom, he shifted to the edge of the chair, braced himself and thrust deeply into her.

The world splintered all around her, sensation on sensation ripping through her until she thought she would die of it, then, with a last defiant thrust, he threw back his head and cried out her name.

Sated, she fell limply against his chest and smoothed the sweat from his brow. 'That was pretty finessey,' she mumbled.

He chuckled, exhausted, and his hands cupped her bottom lovingly and squeezed. 'You're joking. That had all the finesse of a randy adolescent in a hay barn.'

'It felt pretty damn good from here,' she mumbled, almost asleep.

He locked his hands under her bottom and stood, carried her over to the bath, and stepped in, still holding her.

'What are you doing?' she gasped, opening her eyes and staring down at the water.

'Washing you again. You're all soapy still.'

'I'm not surprised— Robert, put me down; we'll fall over.'

She unlocked her legs from his waist and slid them down until her feet touched the bottom of the bath, then they knelt again and washed away the traces of soap and the heady scent of their loving.

'I want you again,' he told her unnecessarily.

She smiled, delighted at his reaction. 'Good. Shall we go to bed this time?'

'For finesse?'

She laughed softly. 'No, for comfort.'

'I had the hard chair,' he pointed out, but he went willingly, she was glad to notice. And it was just as well. By the time they had finished neither of them could move anywhere, and the bed was much more comfortable than the bathroom floor. . .

Jim Pate's leg continued to improve without any further intervention except for the very heavy doses of antibiotics to prevent the possibility of reinfection and to be certain that all traces of the old infection were knocked on the head. His wrist was mending without incident, but because it was fractured he was unable to use crutches and so he had to remain in hospital as he couldn't take any weight on his leg until it had healed.

Joseph Lee, on the other hand, was still showing no sign of forming a callus over the old non-union in his tibia, although the new fracture was healing well. They had opened up the bone ends, filled the gap with chips of cancellous bone and put on an external fixator, then after a fortnight they had sent him home on a strictly non-weight-bearing regime with crutches.

He came back for an outpatient check at six weeks and had a scan, and was very anxious that it should be showing some progress.

However, the bone chips didn't seem to be progressing as fast as Robert wanted them to, and he was frustrated.

'I'm sure I can see a change,' Frankie said thoughtfully as they studied the scan.

'Can you? I'm damned if I can. I think it's wishful thinking.'

'No. Look here. What's that?'

He studied the tiny area she indicated and raised an eyebrow. 'Maybe. It's pretty damn slight if it is an improvement.'

'But surely anything's better than nothing?' she suggested.

He gave a grim laugh. 'If you showed that to Mr

Lee and told him it was getting better you'd be hard pushed to convince him.'

'Even so,' she said, sticking to her guns, 'I think it's getting better.'

'And that, of course, will make all the difference.'

She was exasperated. 'Well, don't you?'

He blew out his breath through pursed lips, then shrugged. 'Perhaps. It's not exactly startling, though, and he's getting very worried about being able to work and look after his wife properly. I think we ought to consider sending him to a specialist centre to have an electrical stimulator implanted if it continues to make so little progress. Maybe that will hustle it up a bit.'

'Can you justify it?'

He shrugged again. 'Not yet, perhaps, but if there isn't any change in, say, another four weeks then I think we can. Hopefully by then time will have proved you right and me wrong. By the way, what are you doing on Friday night?'

'Peeling grapes. Why, are you going to make me a better offer?'

He chuckled. 'There's a Valentine's day ball in aid of the hospital, run by the League of Friends. I wondered if you wanted to go.'

'Do you want to?'

'I thought you might,' he said evasively.

'Do *you* want to?' she repeated more emphatically.

His mouth tipped a little. 'No, not really, I'd rather be at home peeling you grapes.'

She could feel her eyes sparkling. 'I think you just convinced me. Where's Jane for the weekend?'

'She's home for half-term. I pick her up on Friday evening— Oh, damn.'

'No grapes,' Frankie said mournfully.

'To hell with the grapes,' he growled. 'We'll have a week of being on our best behaviour.' He looked longingly at her mouth, then with a frustrated sigh he picked up Mr Lee's notes and tapped them on his other hand. 'Come on, let's tell him how it looks, send him home for four weeks and get on with the clinic,' he said reluctantly.

Jane's half-term was the last complete week in February, and as often happened it snowed, suddenly and without warning.

Robert phoned the hospital to say he was cut off and would be unable to get in until it thawed, and dressed up in his thickest clothes to go out with Jane and build a snowman.

She was too old, really, but then so was he. They had great fun, rolling balls about the garden until they were enormous and then struggling to lift one on top of the other. They found an old tweed cap in the barn, and with the help of a carrot, a slice of orange and some coal they made a face and buttons, then Robert photographed Jane posing by the snowman, her face flushed with the cold and bright with laughter.

Then they went in and made a cup of hot chocolate and sat by the fire, thawing slowly.

Robert was just about to bring up the subject of Frankie and what Jane thought of her when she brought the subject up herself, in a roundabout way.

'It's lovely having you to myself,' she confided.

He was a bit taken aback by that. 'It's lovely to have you,' he said finally. 'You can have no idea how much I've missed having you around all your life. I love you, JJ. Are you happier now you're living here with me?'

She nodded, a little smile on her mouth. 'I love Mum but she's—well—she's not easy to forgive, you know?'

'Yes, I know exactly.' He wound up his nerve a little. 'So, how did you enjoy Center Parcs?'

'Oh, it was brilliant! Can we go again?'

'Maybe.' He looked at his hands, unsure how to go on, but she rattled on ahead of him anyway.

'Frankie's good fun, isn't she? You let her bully you, though.'

He smiled. 'Maybe I like being bullied.'

'Maybe you like having fun, you mean!' She unravelled her legs and crossed over to him, taking his cup out of his hands and putting it down before settling herself on his lap.

'Are you quite comfortable?' he said drily.

'Mmm. I just wanted a hug. It's so nice being here with you on my own. There's always someone around at school, and sometimes it's just nice to be quiet with just the two of us. That's why I love coming here so much.'

He felt a little ripple of apprehension. 'Do you mind Frankie being here sometimes?' he asked cautiously.

'Oh, no, I like her. Still, it's not the same as having you to myself. I can't climb all over you like this when Frankie's here.'

He laughed. 'Why ever not?'

Jane shrugged. 'She'd think I was being silly. Anyway, I'd feel silly.' She shifted until she was looking out of the window. 'Is the snow likely to last long?' she asked wistfully.

'I don't know. Why?'

'Because when it melts the road will be open, and I'll have to share you again.'

With Frankie, he thought, and his heart sank. She didn't like them having a relationship, he realised, and that posed a serious threat to his future happiness with Frankie, because, as he had told her, he and Jane were a package. He'd done enough to hurt her by bringing her into the world so carelessly as a young man. Now, as a responsible and caring adult, the least he could do was ensure her happiness, even if it was at the expense of his own.

Hopefully it wouldn't come to that, and Jane would start to open her heart to Frankie. He couldn't see how she could fail, after all, with Frankie's warm and generous nature. No one could dislike her. He was beginning to think that no one could fail to love her, either—including him.

Jane would come round. She just needed time. . .

The snow didn't last long. By Saturday Jane was fed up with being at home, and Robert, keen to get them together again and give them time to build a relationship, suggested that Frankie should take his daughter shopping again. 'It'll be summer soon, and she'll need other things,' he reasoned. 'And it'll give you time with her again.'

'Sure. You know I'm happy to spend time with her. She's great fun. I love her.'

'So do I—but then she's my daughter,' he said heavily. 'I can't just expect you to like her—or vice versa.'

Frankie looked at him searchingly. 'Robert, has something happened? Has she said something about me?'

He shook his head. 'No—not really. I just get the feeling she might be a little jealous if she realised how deep our relationship was now.'

'Don't you think she ought to know?' Frankie said, worried that they were deceiving Jane, if only by omission.

'No—not yet. Give her time to get to know you. It'll be all right.'

Frankie hoped so. She had the distinct feeling that he wasn't telling her everything, but he might be right. Time with Jane could help to strengthen their friendship. Perhaps then she would be happy to welcome Frankie to the fold.

Jane certainly seemed keen enough to see her on Saturday morning.

'Can we go to Norwich?' she asked her father. 'There are some super shops there.'

'Sure—if Frankie doesn't mind?'

Frankie smiled. 'Frankie doesn't mind. Frankie quite fancies the idea. Do we have a budget?'

He rolled his eyes. 'Just be sensible.'

'When am I ever anything else?' she asked in mock outrage.

He snorted rudely, handed over his cashpoint card and pretended to slit his throat with his finger.

Frankie patted his cheek, kissed him lightly on the mouth and told him not to panic. 'You know you can trust me.'

'Yes, I know,' he murmured. 'I just have visions of all the shopping bags, and it brings me out in a cold sweat. Don't let that stop you having fun, though.'

Frankie laughed and glanced across at Jane. She was staring at them, a curious look on her face, and Frankie had the uneasy feeling that she was withdrawing into herself.

'All ready?' she said brightly.

'Yes.' Just the one word, nothing more.

It was a quiet drive to Norwich, if one discounted the music which Jane put on loudly on Frankie's car radio. Because she liked it, or to drown out any possibility of conversation? Frankie wasn't sure.

However, she soon seemed to perk up once they hit the shops, and Frankie had to all but drag her away at the end of the day.

They hadn't bought as much this time, but Jane had unbent and allowed herself to have fun, and Frankie wondered if Robert was right and she was jealous of their relationship. That night they all went to a film together, and Jane sat in the middle like a chaperon.

She didn't stay after they got back to the house, but said goodnight to both of them at the door and left, declining Robert's invitation for lunch the following day.

She wasn't sure, but she didn't want to come between Jane and her father, and she felt that just now, with all the upheaval of moving up here permanently and the hurtful effect of her mother's behaviour, Jane would need him more than ever.

So she kept out of their way, and she wasn't surprised when Robert knocked on her door on Sunday evening.

'Taken her back?' she asked.

'Mmm. Fancy a quick drink?'

She shook her head. 'Not really. I've missed you. What I want to do is hold you.'

He pushed the door shut behind him and took her in his arms. 'Hold away,' he murmured.

Frankie did, and it was wonderful. 'How's Jane?' she asked through his jumper.

'OK. A bit clingy. I think she's reacting to her mother's stupidity. Now she's safe she can admit that she was hurt by it, poor kid.' He heaved a sigh, and Frankie tipped back her head and kissed him gently.

'You're still angry with her, aren't you?'

'Jackie?' He snorted. 'I feel like killing her sometimes. She rang up the other day—she's short of cash. I'd already sent her a big cheque. She isn't supposed to have maintenance, but I know she used to spend some of JJ's money on herself, and I took it away without warning. She hasn't had a chance to prepare herself or budget for it—not that she would given all the time in the world. She's far too self-centred.'

'No, you're far too soft. I imagine you always have been.'

He sighed. 'Probably. I just wish she'd find some rich count who'd whisk her off to Bavaria or somewhere.'

They shared a rueful smile, and Robert's arms tightened fractionally before releasing her. He stretched out on the bed and bounced his bottom up and down a little.

'God, it is hard and lumpy, isn't it?'

'I said it was.'

'I was just thinking of trying it out, but maybe I'll pass.' He rolled on to his side, propped his head on his hand and grinned. 'Want to come back with me?'

She shook her head, horribly tempted. 'I'd love to, but I'd better not. It's already late. How about a coffee instead?'

His smile was rueful. 'It isn't quite what I had in mind, but if that's all you're offering I'll have to make do with it.'

She chuckled. 'With these walls? Are you kidding? We make far too much noise.'

Just then, to illustrate the point, the man next door came in and turned on his radio.

'You can hear every word!' Robert whispered.

She chuckled. 'I know. Coffee?'

His laugh was wry. 'I think so.'

The next week was hectic. They snatched a couple of hours together on Wednesday evening, but then the phone rang and Robert had to go in, so he took Frankie with him and she went back to her room and lay on her lumpy mattress and missed him.

That week Jim Pate's cast came off his arm, and he was delighted to get rid of it, if a little wary of the unsupported limb.

'It feels so damn thin,' he told Frankie. 'I don't

know, what with the ironmongery on my leg and the cast on my arm I've been a right mess, haven't I?'

Frankie chuckled, hitched a hip up on the edge of his bed and looked down at him in the chair. His leg was supported on a pull-out board, and the rods and screws of the external fixator gleamed at her like some kind of futuristic robot.

'The Bionic Man,' he said with a wry grin. 'Do you think it'll ever be the same again, Frankie?'

She shrugged. 'I don't know. Probably not, but it should be pretty good.'

He stared at it thoughtfully, then started to speak, his voice soft and rather sad. 'I used to be a model, you know. For catalogues and things. It was quite a good living, but then someone smashed my nose and suddenly they didn't want me any more.'

He gave a humourless laugh. 'Nor did anyone else. I'd dropped out of college, my parents wouldn't speak to me—I ended up with nothing. I bummed around London for a while, but then I heard East Anglia was a boom county and I might get a job up here.'

'And?'

He looked up at her with a quick grin. 'They lied. I started living rough, got into prostitution so I could eat, but I got on someone else's patch. That was when my leg got kicked. He tried to kill me. Pity he didn't, really.

'I've done odd jobs since—fruit-picking, digging potatoes, that sort of thing. Casual work for cash, no questions asked. I won't steal, but sometimes it isn't easy. I busk in the subways till I get moved on, and sometimes it's quite good money. Usually, though, it's a case of foraging in the bins outside McDonald's and Burger King—if I can get the left-overs before the rats get them or the bin men come.'

Frankie's brow creased in a quick frown. 'Jim,

that's awful. Don't your parents care?'

He looked blankly at her. 'My parents? I haven't got a clue. They'd think I was just a useless bum, and they'd be right.' He laughed shortly. 'At least I've kept away from drugs. Not even I was that stupid.'

'Why don't you contact them, Jim? They're probably worried sick about you.'

He snorted. 'And pigs fly. No, Frankie. They don't want to know. Dad's a vicar, for God's sake. They've got no room in their home for a useless parasite.'

'I thought Christians taught forgiveness?' she said softly.

His smile was kind and his eyes were centuries old. 'What ever gave you that idea, Frankie Bradley?'

He looked away, his eyes suddenly bright, and Frankie gave in to impulse and hugged him hard.

'Contact them, Jim, please? At least let them know you're alive?'

He shrugged her off, his shoulders stiff, and she let go and straightened up. 'At least tell me you'll think about it.'

'I have thought about it,' he told her gruffly. 'I've thought about precious little else for the last six years, but it's too late now. Circles close, Frankie. There's no place for me there now.'

'You're wrong, Jim,' she said quietly. 'There's no family circle in the world that would close so tight that a prodigal son couldn't return.'

He looked at her again, and she saw tears wet on his cheeks. 'There's no such thing as a fatted calf; I learned that years ago. I knew the rules—I chose not to play by them. I've got no one to blame but myself.' He reached out and took her hand. 'I'm OK, Frankie. I'll survive, don't you worry about me.'

But she did—endlessly. She wanted to talk to Robert, but he had Jackie for the weekend so she could see Jane, and she gathered from the atmosphere when he popped in on Saturday that it was not going well.

She was walking out of the kitchen opposite her room with a cup of coffee in her hand when Gavin Jones came in, bumping into her and slopping the coffee over her hand.

'Ouch!' she exclaimed, and, putting the cup down, she ran her hand under the tap.

'Are you all right?'

She grinned at Gavin. 'I'll live. Cold water will sort it out; it wasn't that hot.'

He blotted up the floor with a paper towel and propped himself against the worktop, watching her as she held her hand in the cold running water.

'So, how are things? Think you'll make the grade?'

She smiled. 'He says so.'

'Of course, he has a vested interest. I don't imagine he wants you to leave under the circumstances.'

'Circumstances?' she said, paying undue attention to her hand.

'I'm sorry, I'm gossiping. Forget it.'

She gave a strained laugh. 'Does everyone know?'

'Probably. Hospitals are like that. Does it matter?'

She thought about it. 'No, not really. His daughter doesn't know yet.'

Gavin raised one eyebrow. 'Really? Well, she won't find out from me.' He turned off the tap, pulled her hand round into the light and studied it carefully.

'Well, Doctor?'

He grinned and released her. 'It looks OK. I was just about to make myself one—want to join me?'

Suddenly she had an overwhelming urge for his company. He was kind, generous, thoughtful and funny, his friendship just exactly that. He obviously knew the situation with her and Robert, so there would be no tacky fending-off and hurt feelings.

'Thanks,' she told him. 'I will.'

His room was no more comfortable than her own, the bed just as lumpy, the furniture just as spartan. 'Any sign of your flat yet?' she asked.

He smiled ruefully. 'I haven't had time to look, to be honest. Well, that's not true, but the estate agents tend to work normal hours, and that's when I'm on duty—for starters. It's hard to catch them between midnight and five a.m. on a Sunday morning, and I usually have better things to do, like sleeping.'

He lay across the top of the bed, his feet propped on the bedside table, and looked around the room. 'Pretty dire, isn't it? Still, I keep thinking, It's only temporary, so what does it matter?' He laughed. 'So, Dr Bradley, tell me what you've learned this week.'

'Well,' she said slowly, 'I've done a patellectomy—that's removing a kneecap.'

He arched a brow. 'I did know that.'

She laughed. 'Sorry. I didn't till I did, if you know what I mean. I've done a knee replacement, prescribed quite the wrong treatment for a burst fracture of a thoracic vertebra and been stopped in my tracks, fortunately, and plated a nasty ankle. Oh, and three hip replacements and a couple of arthroscopies.'

'Quite old hat,' he said with a grin.

'Absolutely. Actually, there's one person I am worried about. He's a drop-out—well, I think in fact society dropped him out when he fell on hard times. He's had chronic osteomyelitis and he hasn't got anywhere to live. I'm so worried he'll go back to the old warehouse he was living in down by the river—it'll be cold and damp, filthy. We can't keep him in indefinitely, but he's got nowhere else.'

'The council will find him a hostel,' Gavin told her.

'Don't worry, they have contingency plans for these old boys.'

'But he's not old; that's just it. He's only twenty-six, and his life's all ahead of him. I tried to get him to contact his parents, but he won't because he says they'll want nothing to do with him. His father's a vicar, for goodness' sake!'

'In which case he's probably right. It would set the parish council by the ears if the vicar's son crawled back covered in the slime of society's gutters.'

She stared down into her coffee. 'He's so sad, Gavin. He desperately wants to go home.'

'Oh, Frankie,' Gavin said softly. 'You want to put the world to rights and it won't have any of it. Believe me. I've tried. Now I just keep my nose down and stay out of it. Other people's problems are their own.'

She stared at him. 'Gavin, you don't mean that. You sound just like Jim Pate.'

'Your drop-out?' His smile was wry. 'I expect we went to the same school of hard knocks—we were just in a different class. Trust me, Frankie, he's right. His folks don't want him. He's following a different drummer and they don't understand the rhythm.'

She went back to her room and thought of Jim Pate and his parents, and Robert's wife Jackie. She was certainly following a different drummer—and understanding her took some doing.

Maybe Gavin was right. People's problems were their own, and she should stay out of Jim's and let him get on with it. . .

CHAPTER NINE

IT WAS early March, and spring was beginning to touch the landscape with green. Buds were bursting on the trees, and everywhere daffodils nodded their heads in cheerful profusion.

Frankie hardly had time to notice. Robert was delegating more and more responsibility, because David Hunt's father was ill again and he had taken some leave to be with him. Robert was therefore busier, and the knock-on effect meant that Frankie hardly had time to turn round.

When she wasn't on duty, though, she was with Robert, and although she had never spent the night there there had been times when the milkmen were out as she was on her way back to the hospital.

He still hadn't told her that he loved her, but his lovemaking was so tender, so caring and sensitive that she knew he must.

He was withdrawn, though, and she sensed he was keeping something from her—something she wouldn't want to hear.

She began to wonder why he hadn't told Jane about the change in their relationship, but then it occurred to her that perhaps she had failed the test. Perhaps Jane had said she didn't like her, and so Frankie wasn't considered good enough. He didn't love her, so although he would keep her on as a mistress for as long as it suited him he wouldn't bother to distress his daughter with her father's human needs and frailties.

She decided to have one last go at persuading him

to talk to Jane. If he refused, then she would have to believe in her instincts, in which case there was no point in staying here. She wouldn't make herself a doormat for anyone, no matter how worthy they might seem.

On the second Monday in March, Jim Pate was discharged into the care of the local authority, who were to house him in a hostel and care for him until he was fit.

Frankie had grave doubts about his discharge, but, as Robert said, they couldn't keep him for ever.

'I hope he's all right,' she said, biting her lip as she watched him go.

'So do I,' Robert said heavily. 'He'll be back for check-ups. We'll keep an eye on the situation. If it looks too dodgy I'm sure we can readmit him.'

'On what grounds?'

He grinned at her. 'I'll think of something. Mr Lee's in this afternoon for a scan and check-up. I wonder which of us was right?'

Frankie shook her head. 'You, I expect, although I hope it was me. I'd be so pleased if that leg had started to heal.'

'You and me both, Dr Bradley—you and me both. I'll tell you what.'

'What?'

'If you're right, I'll take you out for dinner on Friday night—a really super slap-up meal. It's time we did that.'

'And if I'm wrong?'

He grinned. 'I'll take me out instead—only I'll need company, of course.'

She laughed softly. 'Sounds like you've got it all worked out, Mr Ryder.'

'Sure have,' he chuckled.

They went down to the orthopaedic clinic that afternoon, and together they looked at the results of the scan.

Frankie punched the air. 'Yes! I get dinner!'

'You were getting dinner anyway,' Robert reminded her drily. 'Well done, though. You were right. It's healing well, and within a few weeks he should be fine. Let's go and tell him the good news.'

Mr Lee was, naturally, delighted. 'Well, to be honest I thought I was stuck with that awful pain for ever,' he confessed with a chuckle. 'Oh, May will be so thrilled.'

'How is she?' Frankie asked.

'Oh, doing a bit better now. She's got a bad chest, and every winter it seems to get worse, but the spring's here now. Things will soon be better.'

Frankie grinned at him. 'Do you know, Mr Lee,' she said, 'I think you might be right?'

For the rest of the week, although busy, Frankie was happy. Darren Hawkes came back to have his ankle checked, and she was over the moon with the result of his skin graft. It looked a million times better, she thought, and not nearly as awful as she had imagined it would.

The patient with the burst fracture of the vertebra was doing well on Robert's regime of strict bed rest for six weeks followed by gentle mobilisation. So far a fortnight had passed, and the patient was in considerably less pain.

The neurological damage was slight, restricted to a slight loss of sensation along one nerve root pathway, and the patient would probably make a total recovery—much better than her plan to mobilise immediately, because she had missed the slight sensation loss.

It was a serious error, and one she had berated herself for over and over again.

Robert had repeated his claim that no one could be perfect all of the time, and that a few mistakes like that which were picked up did no one any harm and helped the learning process.

That was certainly true! Her learning curve had acquired a real kink in it after that!

Friday night finally arrived. The other team were on call, their patients were covered for the weekend and Jane was going to a friend's house for the weekend.

'Why don't you stay?' Robert suggested. 'Bring some things with you and we'll make a weekend of it. It seems to have been ages since we were together for more than a few minutes.'

So she agreed, and later, having put on the dress she had bought with Jane, she picked up her little overnight bag, loaded it in her car and left for Robert's.

He came out to meet her, drawing her into his arms as soon as she was out of the car and kissing her lingeringly.

'Hell, Frankie, I've missed you,' he murmured against her hair.

Her arms tightened around him almost convulsively. 'I've missed you too,' she replied, choked. 'It's been so long since I've held you like this.'

'Too long. Come on in; it's cold. I've got the fire going, the kettle's on and we can have a coffee before we leave.' He took her bag from her, slung his arm round her shoulders and shepherded her into the house.

They nearly didn't get out of the door, of course, because she took her coat off and Robert groaned. 'Not that wicked, delectable dress?' he muttered. 'Frankie, how could you do that to me? Come here. . .'

She went, but only briefly. He was too tempting himself in dark suit-trousers and a fine silk shirt. He hadn't put his tie on yet, and that wretched curl was lurking there, in the V. . .

She tweaked it, and he winced and met her eyes. 'You're a wicked hussy,' he said gruffly. 'I think we ought to skip the coffee and go. We can have a drink there.'

He put his tie on, and she stood behind him at the mirror and slid her hands into his pockets. He grinned and jackknifed. 'Get out, woman; that tickles.'

She smiled her siren's smile. 'No. I'm having fun.' She delved a little deeper, and he groaned and leaned against her, their eyes meeting in the mirror.

'Is that something in your pocket, or are you pleased to see me?' she murmured, and he gave a choking laugh and turned, pulling her into his arms.

'You are a wicked, wicked woman,' he murmured against her lips.

'Mmm. Robert?'

'Mmm?'

'Are we going out?'

'I suppose so. I don't want to, but I did promise you a slap-up meal, so I suppose we ought to.'

'We could stay in and have cheese on toast.'

'I've booked the table.'

'Oh.' She moved away from him reluctantly, smiling that smile. 'We'd better go, then. My coat, please?'

He helped her into it, settled it round her shoulders and then shrugged into his jacket. He didn't bother with a coat. 'It'll do me good to cool down,' he said with a wry grin when she questioned it.

They drove to the restaurant, a little place tucked away in the country with a very intimate feel, very much as if they were being entertained in someone's home. They were seated in front of a roaring log fire on a comfortable old settee, drinks were brought to them by the owner on an antique silver tray and they sat sipping their drinks and nibbling nuts and trying to keep their hands off each other.

In the end Robert gave up, took Frankie's hand in his and snuggled it against his thigh. 'I don't care if anyone sees us,' he said. 'Who said romance was dead?'

Not Frankie. He might not come out with gratuitous compliments all the time, but, whenever they were alone, by look or touch or word he was more romantic than anyone she had ever met. He made her feel truly feminine, very much desired, and all woman.

And tonight was no exception. He was warm and funny, their conversation sparkled, and beneath it all was the undercurrent of passion simmering almost out of control.

Anticipation. That was the thing, she decided. The meal was almost a courtship ritual, the dessert a foregone conclusion, but the stylised delay was what tantalised.

As if he knew that, Robert played his part to the full. They didn't eat a great deal—Frankie found it impossible to force much past the tightness in her throat and Robert's appetite was clearly not for the food, however delicious.

They lingered, though, savouring each course, driving the tension higher and higher.

Finally, when Frankie thought she was going to scream, he surrendered.

Setting his coffee down with exaggerated care, he turned to the proprietor. 'Could I have the bill, please?' he asked.

He paid by credit card, and moments later he was helping her on with her coat, settling her into the car and sliding behind the wheel.

'That was a wonderful meal,' she said in the tense, electric silence.

'Wasn't it?' He glanced across at her, their faces lit by the soft glow from the welcoming lights of the restaurant. 'You look beautiful tonight.'

Her hand reached out and she laid her fingers against his jaw, feeling the tension. 'So do you.'

Their eyes locked, their breathing became light and shallow, and with a little shake of his head Robert turned and started the engine.

The drive home was silent but mercifully short. He let them in, kicked the door shut and she went into his waiting arms.

'I need you,' he muttered darkly. 'Frankie?'

His hands pushed off her coat and she put her arms behind her and let it fall. His jacket was next, then the tie, then their shoes.

'This is crazy,' he said, and, picking her up in his arms, he carried her up the stairs to his bedroom and set her on her feet, lowering her slowly down his body for maximum effect.

They were both trembling, the buttons of his shirt too much for them. He managed the top two and his cuff-links, then wrenched it over his head. Something ripped but he didn't pause, throwing it aside and turning back to Frankie.

'Take off your dress,' he said hoarsely. 'Nice and slow.'

Her pulse hammering, she picked up the hem and drew the dress up over her head.

His breath caught. 'Dammit, Frankie, if I'd known you were wearing that you would never have got out of the door this evening.'

She held the dress at arm's length and dropped it. 'You approve?' she asked, her voice husky with desire.

His eyes scorched over her, over the pale cream of the lace teddy, the suspenders, the sheer Lycra stockings, and then came back to her face.

'Approve?' he muttered. 'Lord, woman, if you had the slightest idea. . .'

'Your turn.'

He didn't take his eyes off her as he stripped off the rest of his clothes and flung them anywhere. His watch was last, dropped on the floor without a thought.

'Take off the stockings,' he said tightly.

She did, rolling them down slowly and deliberately, first one, then the other.

The teddy was next. She made him undo the snaps, so intimately placed, and his hands trembled against her thighs. She bent forward and laid a feather-soft kiss against his skin, and he jumped as if she'd shot him.

'Take it off,' he gritted.

She dropped the straps, slid it down over her hips and wriggled out of it.

'Now what?' she said teasingly.

'Now I'm going to make you pay for that,' he growled softly. He stripped back the quilt, ordered her to lie down and then slowly, systematically, he started at her head and worked his way down to her feet, kissing every inch.

By the time he reached her toes she was almost beside herself. His tongue was hot, wickedly clever and more than she could bear, and suddenly she couldn't stand it any more. She sat up, her hands reaching for him, and pleaded with him incoherently.

He moved up beside her again, his hand trailing fire over her thighs, and then, grasping her wrists in one hand, he moved over her and hovered, tantalising her yet again.

'Say please,' he taunted, but his voice was uneven, his body was trembling and even as she said the word he was crumbling, his resolve swept away by the fierce passion that rode them.

She thought he would be rough, the suspense too

much for them both, but he wasn't; his body racked with the effort of control, he moved slowly, gently, as if he couldn't bear the thought of it being over and so was prolonging it for as long as he could.

Finally, though, his control snapped and he released her wrists, dropped his face into her shoulder and groaned. 'Frankie, come with me,' he whispered, and then he took off the brakes.

It was a wild, tempestuous ride, short but devastating in its impact, like a runaway roller coaster.

As they climbed the last peak and fell headlong down the final run, Frankie sobbed and clung to him, her face buried in his neck, her arms locked round him as if she would never let him go.

He collapsed against her, his chest heaving, and as the pounding of his heart slowed he levered himself up and looked down into her swimming eyes.

'What ever are you going to do for an *encore*?' she murmured, and with a choked laugh he fell beside her, pulled her into his arms and cradled her against his heart.

Within moments they were asleep.

Frankie opened her eyes slowly. Dragging herself out of sleep, she became aware of three things.

One, the sun was pouring in.

Two, the quilt had slipped to their waists.

Three, the noise that had woken her was Jane's voice, calling out for Robert, who was sprawled naked beside her, fast asleep.

She shook him. 'Robert, it's Jane! She's here!' she whispered, frantically dragging up the quilt.

His eyes opened at the same time as the bedroom door, and widened as Jane took one step into the room, stopped in her tracks and gasped.

'Dad?' she said uncertainly, gazing around at the

clothes strewn across the floor where they had dropped them in the heat of their passion.

'Oh, God!' she sobbed, clapping her hand over her mouth, and then she spun on her heel and ran. They heard her fall on the stairs and give a startled cry, then the door opened and slammed, and Robert was out of bed, dragging on his trousers and running after her in bare feet, out onto the frosty gravel.

Frankie didn't hurry. She thought they needed time together, time to deal with the sudden revelation and its implications.

She went along to the bathroom, washed briefly and took off last night's make-up, then went back to the bedroom, dressed in jeans and a jumper and packed away the rest of her things. In a sort of icy calm she put Robert's clothes in the laundry basket, picked up his watch and laid it on the bedside table, then went downstairs.

They were in the kitchen, Jane slumped across the table in floods of tears, Robert standing helplessly nearby dressed only in his trousers, ramming his hands through his hair.

He looked up at Frankie, his eyes pleading. 'I can't reason with her,' he told her unsteadily. 'She just keeps calling me a bastard.'

Frankie put the kettle on. 'I think we should all sit down and have a cup of tea and talk about this like reasonable human beings, don't you?'

Jane lifted her tear-stained face and looked at Frankie with such hurt in her eyes that she could have wept.

'I thought you were my friend,' she said tearfully, her voice rising. 'I thought I could trust you, but you're just like my mother—' She broke off, a sob convulsing her chest, her slim hand pressed over her mouth to hold in the pain.

Frankie bit her lip, unable to bear it. 'Oh, Jane, that isn't true—'

'Don't lie to me! I saw you! Look at the place—clothes everywhere, ripped off each other like animals—'

'Jane, that's enough,' Robert ordered. 'Apologise to Frankie immediately.'

'Why should I?' The girl's eyes swivelled to her father, and another tear slid down her cheek and splashed onto the table. 'I thought you were different. I thought I could trust you, that I was safe with you, but you're all the same, all of you, at it like rabbits—'

She leapt up and ran out, through the back door and down the garden to the swing at the end.

Frankie caught Robert's arm as he made to follow her.

'Let her go. She needs to cry, to get it out of her system. When she's calmed down you can talk to her.'

He stared down the garden, his eyes filled with tears of remorse. 'I've failed her, Frankie. I knew she was worried about our relationship. I think she felt threatened by you, as if there was only room for one of you. I was going to talk to her tomorrow—pick her up from her friend's and sit down with her and see if I could make her understand—'

He broke off, his face contorted with regret. Frankie put her arms round him to comfort him but he moved away. 'I'm sorry,' he muttered. 'I just—' He shook his head, unable to find the words.

'I'll go,' Frankie said quietly, her heart heavy. There was nothing she could say or do. It was between Robert and his daughter, and she was just in the way.

She laid a hand on his shoulder. 'Call me later,' she said, but he didn't move or reply, his eyes fixed on Jane, weeping at the end of the garden.

She let herself out, put her bag in the car and drove

back to the hospital. She almost made it to her room before the tears came.

A moment later there was a knock on the door.

She scrubbed her cheeks. 'Who is it?' she said, her voice clogged with tears. The door opened.

'Want a shoulder?' Gavin offered gently.

'Oh, Gavin—'

He gathered her gently into his arms, rocked her against his chest and let her cry.

'Now,' he murmured as she hiccuped to a halt, 'tell Uncle Gavin all about it.'

She wiped the tears from her eyes, blew her nose on the tissue he pushed into her hand and then shredded it into her lap.

'His daughter came back.'

'Oh.'

'We were still in bed. She didn't know that we were—you know—having an affair.' She looked up at the ceiling and drew a shaky breath, then closed her eyes. 'It was awful, Gavin,' she whispered. 'I felt as if I'd let her down. He should have told her. She should have known about us. He was going to tell her tomorrow, and now it's too late to do it gently.' She took a steadying breath. 'Can you imagine how she must feel?'

'Coming face to face with your parents' sexuality is all part of growing up,' he told her gently. 'She'll get over it.'

Frankie shook her head. 'I don't know. Really, Gavin, I don't know. She's had more to contend with than most children of her age. I think this will take a lot of getting over.'

'Then she'll need time.' He patted her shoulder and stood up. 'Have you had breakfast?' She shook her head. 'Come on, then. Wash your face and we'll go and pig out in the canteen.'

'I couldn't.'

'No such word. Come on. You've got five minutes before I break in here and carry you up the corridor.'

She gave a tearful chuckle.

'That's better. Five minutes, now.'

He was wonderful. He kept her going throughout that long and awful day, but despite his best efforts she couldn't shake off the awful dread.

Robert rang her late that night, his voice guarded.

'How is she?' Frankie forced herself to ask.

'Angry, hurt, betrayed. She's angry with you as much as with me. She says you pretended to be her friend, and all the time you were using her to suck up to me.'

Frankie closed her eyes. 'Oh, Robert, that isn't true.'

'I know. I can't convince her, though. She'll hardly speak to me. She says she came over this morning because she fell out with her friend and wanted to be with me, so she borrowed some money off the mother and caught the train.'

'But it's miles from the station!'

'She walked—it took her half an hour; she got a lift some of the way.'

'She hitched?' Frankie was appalled.

'Don't worry,' Robert said grimly. 'She won't do that again. I'll try and have another talk with her tomorrow before I take her back to school, but she's not very happy with me. She says she's going back to live with her mother—says at least Jackie never lied to her.'

Frankie's eyes closed in despair. 'Oh, Robert, you can't let her—'

'I know. Don't worry, Frankie, I'll make sure she's all right. I'll speak to you tomorrow.'

He rang her at ten, just as she was about to ring him.

'How are things?' she asked directly.

'Grim. She still won't talk to me. I'll give her the

week to settle down, then try again. I've told the school—that was an experience I don't wish to repeat. I was made to feel like an irresponsible teenager, but I thought they should know there was something wrong.'

'I'm sure they should,' Frankie agreed.

He didn't linger on the phone. There was little to say that hadn't been said before, and only time would change things.

That week they were busy. Robert spoke to Jane on the phone, but again she wouldn't talk to him and got upset.

He looked awful, his face grey and drawn, his eyes troubled, and as the weekend approached his temper grew worse and worse.

As if by mutual consent he and Frankie didn't spend any time together except at the hospital. They were both too distressed by Jane's unhappiness to pursue their own pleasure, and when Friday came Frankie was on duty anyway, and worked all weekend.

She thought it would take her mind off what was going on at Robert's house, but it simply blunted the edges. Underneath she was conscious, through all she did, of a knot of tension and pain that wouldn't go away.

Robert had promised to come and see her on Sunday after he took Jane back, and it was the longest forty-eight hours of her life. When she heard the quick footfall outside her door at nine on Sunday evening, she could hardly open the door for the dread filling her.

He came in, stared at her for a moment and then, with a ragged groan, pulled her into his arms.

'How is she?' she mumbled into his jacket.

He released her and paced to the window, staring out into the blackness. 'Miserable. She still won't talk about it properly. I don't know how to reach her.'

'I don't think you can,' she said, curling up on the bed. 'She needs to come to you, and you'll just have to wait. Sit down and tell me all about it.'

He perched on the edge of the bed, his hand over her feet, his head bowed. 'I didn't tell her it was getting serious between us because I knew there'd be an almighty scene and I didn't know how to deal with it. In the end, of course, I did the worst possible thing.'

His fingers traced her toes, his mind miles away, his voice filled with self-disgust. 'I'm not really used to being a parent—I haven't had much chance—and now I've been flung in at the deep end and I've made a total foul-up of it.'

She covered his hand with hers and squeezed it comfortingly. 'She'll come round, Robert, if you give her time.'

He looked at her, his eyes bleak, and then she knew. 'I don't think so,' he said heavily. 'The last thing she said to me was that she never wanted to see you again.'

Frankie took a steadying breath. 'She's upset, Robert. She feels let down.'

'And it's my fault.' He took her hand in his and held it as if his life depended on it. 'Frankie, I asked her to try and understand how we felt. Her reply was what about us understanding how *she* felt.' He stared blankly out of the window. 'She asked me to promise that I wouldn't carry on seeing you outside work.'

Frankie's mouth felt dry, like cotton wool. She had to force the words out. 'And did you?' she asked.

He looked at her, and his eyes were a welter of emotions. 'Frankie, I had to. She has to come first, even if that means—'

He broke off, gripping her hand, and took a shuddering breath. 'It has to work for us both, Frankie. I can't sacrifice Jane's happiness for my own—you know that. She's part of me, the most important part. I'm sorry.'

He stood up and looked down at her, his voice raw with pain. 'I'd better go. Thank you for everything you've given me. Thank you for your warmth, for your love. You'll never know what it meant. . .'

She couldn't move, couldn't speak. If she opened her mouth it would be to beg him to stay, to make love to her one last time.

She couldn't do that, not to Jane, or Robert, or to herself.

So she let him go, her heart breaking, and only when the door was closed did she let the bitter tears fall. . .

CHAPTER TEN

WITHOUT Gavin's support the next week would have been unbearable. He said nothing, just let her talk if she wanted to, gave her a shoulder to cry on and fed her in between.

Fortunately they were busy. David Hunt's father had died the same awful weekend, and so in David's absence Robert and Frankie were too busy for anything other than very brief, technical exchanges about treatment.

However, she found time for one other conversation with him. He was in his office dealing with some of the paperwork when she went in.

He glanced up, put down what he was doing and sat back.

'Have a seat.'

She declined, instead walking over to the window to see if she could draw inspiration from the trees in the distance, beyond the sprawl of the hospital she had grown to know so well.

'I'm leaving at the end of the week,' she told him quietly.

He was silent for a long while, then she heard an untidy sigh. 'I guessed you might,' he said, his voice heavy. 'The hospital will miss you. You've been an excellent member of the team.' He cleared his throat. 'You know you can rely on me for references, don't you?'

She gave a tiny spurt of laughter that was halfway to a sob. 'Just so long as they don't find out about us. You're hardly impartial, after all.' Even though he didn't love her, she thought. He had never said so. He was fond of her, she knew that. Maybe Jane's objection had been convenient, in a way, releasing him from an affair that had been threatening to become too serious?

She dragged in a breath and turned to face him. 'I'll miss you,' she told him honestly. 'You've taught me a lot. I won't forget it, or the fact that you didn't want me at first.'

He laughed without humour. 'Oh, I wanted you, Frankie. That was the trouble. The other applicant was only very average. He was just less of a threat to my peace of mind.'

'It's a pity you didn't have him, really,' Frankie said sadly. 'Then none of this would have happened.'

He opened his mouth to say something but her bleeper squawked, and, excusing herself, she left his office and went back to the ward. She didn't trust herself to use the phone in his office. It was altogether too close to him and she was too near to tears to cope.

Medically, she supposed at the end of that week, she was leaving on a high note. Mr Lee's leg had finally shown signs of healing well, Darren Hawkes' foot was making good progress with her skin grafts on, and she knew that her surgical skills had improved enormously.

Only one patient worried her, and that was Jim Pate. He hadn't turned up for his outpatient appointment, and she felt she couldn't leave without finding out what had happened to him. However, when she rang the hostel on Sunday afternoon she was told that he'd left a week before.

'His father came and they had a row. He left after that,' the girl she spoke to told her. 'His father was ever so upset. He came back later and tried to talk to him, but he'd gone. He left a number—do you want it?'

Frankie did. She rang it and asked for Mr Pate, and a few moments later a quietly spoken man came on the line. 'Gordon Pate here—can I help you?' he said kindly.

'Hello. My name's Frances Bradley. Mr Pate, it's about your son. I'm the doctor who's been treating him, and I'm concerned about him. I gather you saw him a few days ago.'

'James? How is he? Is he all right? What's happened?'

She could hear the note of panic in his voice and hastened to reasure him. 'I don't know,' she said calmingly. 'Nothing that I'm aware of, but he didn't attend his outpatient appointment. I just wondered if you had any idea where he might have gone.'

'No, none. Dr Bradley, if you find him, could you give him a message from me? Could you tell him we love him and want him home? Tell him we're praying for him.'

'I will,' Frankie assured him.

'Ask him to phone—and if he won't I'd be so grateful if you could, just to put our minds at rest. We've been so worried for so long. . .'

'Don't worry, Mr Pate, I'm sure he'll be all right,' Frankie said soothingly. 'I'll pass your message on, and I'll ring you anyway. Bye.'

'Goodbye, Dr Bradley—and be careful,' the man said as she put the phone down.

She glanced at her watch. It was four o'clock—still over two hours of daylight left. She'd just got time to check out her hunch.

She went back to her room, scribbled a note for Gavin and pushed it under his door, then ran to her car.

If she was right, she'd find him down by the river, in a disused warehouse—but where? She made her way down to the docks and started cruising along, looking about for any sign of him or any other human being.

The light was failing and she was about to give up when she saw a sign up ahead. 'Dockside Development Company', it read. 'One- and two-bedroomed apartments'.

'Bijou little apartments for would-be yuppies', was how Jim had described them. There was no sign of work having started, though, so maybe he was still here.

She parked her car and walked slowly towards the building. There was a huge sliding roller-shutter, rusted and peeling, and beside it a personnel door hung open, its hinges broken and creaking in the wind. She stepped cautiously inside.

'Jim?' she called. 'Jim, are you here?'

'Frankie, get out! Run—aagh!'

She heard a thud, a scream, and then she was running, not out but into the darkened warehouse, following the sound of the noise through the abandoned crates that littered the floor.

She saw Jim, lying on the ground while someone kicked him in the ribs, and she ran over and grabbed the man by the shoulders, dragging him back.

'Stop it! For God's sake stop it! You'll kill him!'

'Smart, ain't she?' someone sneered.

She grabbed at the man who was kicking Jim again, and begged him to stop. 'I'm a doctor, for heaven's sake! I can't let you do this!'

'She can't let us, boys,' the same sneering voice said. 'You'll have to stop—the lady said so.'

They laughed, an evil, jeering gang of about three,

she thought, or maybe four. She turned to see the ringleader's face and felt a fist jar against her cheek, sending her staggering back.

Another fist landed in her back, winding her, and then she felt a boot connect with her hip and she screamed.

'Mr Ryder? It's Gavin Jones. I don't want to worry you but I'm a bit concerned about Frankie. I think she could be in trouble.'

Robert jerked up straight in the chair, his attention caught instantly. 'Frankie? What sort of trouble?'

'I don't know. You know the drop-out, Jim Pate? He didn't come to her clinic the other day and she's worried about him. I've just come back and found a note under my door saying that if she's not back by six I should ring the police. She's down at the docks, it says, looking for a warehouse on the river. It's about to be redeveloped into flats or something, I remember her saying.'

Robert looked at his watch. It was only five-thirty, but still. . . 'Phone the police. I'm on my way down there. Tell them everything you know, and get them to hurry.'

He grabbed a jacket and his keys and ran for the door.

'I want to come,' Jane said, her eyes wide and frightened.

'No, stay here—and for once in your life do as you're told. I can't worry about both of you.'

He ran to the car, gunned the engine and shot off down the drive in a flurry of gravel. Where the hell on the docks? He had seen a warehouse waiting for conversion. He could picture it—the pitch of the roof and the old dormer windows of the offices in the top. He tried to remember, to picture the location, but all he could remember was thinking that the smell of gas would put people off—

That was it! The gasometer! He headed through town, using his car phone to contact the police and tell them his hunch, then he turned onto the old dockfront, put his foot down and raced along the rough, uneven ground.

He reached the end, turned sharp right and there in the distance he saw her car. 'Thank God,' he muttered, and, skidding to a halt beside it, he leapt out and ran for the open door into the building.

Then he heard her scream.

'Frankie?' he yelled. 'Frankie, where are you?'

He darted between the scattered crates, searching the darkness for any sign of her.

There was a muffled scream and a dull thud, and he spun towards the noise. 'Frankie?'

Someone cursed, and then she screamed his name, the sound cut off abruptly, but it was enough. He could make them out now in the dark, and, running towards them, he picked up a broken piece of packing case and brought it down hard on the head of the man holding Frankie.

He dropped in his tracks, releasing her, and Robert spun round and swung the lump of wood into the midsection of another man coming at him from behind. He folded over with a grunt, and then Robert heard a slight noise and looked up just as Gavin brought one of Jim's aluminium crutches down on the last man's arm.

He screamed in pain and the knife dropped with a clatter at Robert's feet just as the police sirens screamed to a halt outside and the pounding of feet brought reinforcements in.

'Here come the cavalry,' Gavin said, puffing slightly. 'I think I might have broken his arm.'

'Good,' Robert replied, and picked up the knife. Powerful torches sliced through the air, homed in on them and then they were surrounded by police. 'All right, everyone, let's get this sorted out. What's going on here?'

'Officer, could you please arrest these men for assault?' Robert said.

The policeman in front looked from Robert to the three groaning men and raised an eyebrow. 'Who are you? Superman?' he asked drily, and then turned back to the muggers.

'All right, you lot. I might have known it was you. Look who we've got here, boys—our old friend Smiley. What's it all about, eh, Smiley? We've been watching you, son, and we don't like what you've been doing. Call the drugs squad, please, Sergeant. Let's get these boxes opened.'

Robert handed the knife to the policeman and dropped to his knees beside Frankie, reaching out a trembling hand to touch her face. 'Frankie? Are you all right? For God's sake talk to me!'

'Jim,' she mumbled. 'How's Jim?'

Robert glanced up. 'Gavin's looking after him. Where do you hurt?'

Her little laugh tore through him. 'Everywhere. My lip, my eye—cheekbone, really. My hip and ribs—' She gave a shuddering little sob, and with enormous care he gathered her into his arms and rocked her gently.

'It's all right, Frankie. You're OK now. It's all over.'

'Jim's OK,' Gavin said from beside them. 'He's had a bit of a kicking but he'll live. I think he needs admitting, though, because that fixator looks a bit bent. I suspect he's going to be rather sore for a few days.'

'I've called an ambulance,' the policeman told them. 'We'll take this lot down to the station, charge them and then get a statement off these two at the hospital. Damn drop-outs—they're more trouble than they're worth.' He looked down at Frankie. 'She's new.'

'She's a doctor—she came to look for Jim,' Gavin told him. 'He probably owes her his life.'

'Bloody fool she is, then,' he said. 'He's not worth it.'

'His father thinks he is,' she mumbled thickly through her injured mouth. 'He wants him to go home.'

'Good. That's one less for us to worry about.'

'I think these men could do with being looked at— the suit probably has a broken arm,' Gavin advised.

'Serves him right. Pity it wasn't his neck,' the policeman growled. 'All right, let's get you out of here.'

The three men were taken out to the waiting police cars and driven off just as the ambulance arrived. Jim was loaded into it, but Robert wouldn't let Frankie out of his sight.

'I'll take her,' he said, and followed the ambulance to the hospital. All the way there Frankie lay back against the seat, her eyes closed, hands tightly clasped in her lap. He couldn't really see her face, but what he had seen of it made him want to murder the person or persons responsible.

He reached out a hand and laid it over hers, and she seized it and wouldn't let go. Thank God for automatics, he thought as he drove one-handed back to the hospital.

When they arrived he prised his fingers free and helped her out of the car, leading her into A and E.

Anna Haddon, the staff nurse, was on duty, and, tutting under her breath, she put her arm round Frankie and led her straight round the back. 'Let's have a look at you, sweetheart,' she said gently. 'What happened?'

She glanced over her shoulder at Robert, realised he wasn't going anywhere, and ignored him, stripping Frankie quickly and checking her for wounds. 'Just bruising, I think, but you'll need X-rays. I'll get Patrick to look at you.'

She covered Frankie with a blanket and slipped out, coming back a moment later with her husband, who felt very gently over Frankie's face, frowned at her bruised ribs and hip and agreed with Anna. 'Photos of the ribs and the cheekbone, I think, but just as a precaution. Then you need ice on that nasty bump and on your lip, a good stiff drink and an early night. Have you got anyone to look after you?'

'I'll look after her,' Robert said firmly.

Patrick nodded, satisfied, and then filled in the forms. 'Queue-jump, please. She doesn't need to hang about. She's had a nasty experience.'

Anna took Frankie through to X-Ray in a gown, brought her back and then Patrick looked at the plates with Robert peering over his shoulder just to make sure he didn't miss anything.

'All right?' he said, and Robert gave a slight smile.

'Yes, she's all right. I'll take her home. The police can talk to her tomorrow—doctor's orders.'

He dressed her again, his hands infinitely gentle, and then walked her carefully back to the car, helped her in and drove her slowly back to his house.

Frankie hurt everywhere. Her hip hurt when she put weight on that leg, her ribs hurt every time she breathed, her lip felt enormous and her cheekbone was throbbing with agony.

Robert led her gently into the kitchen, pushed her into a chair and eased off her coat, then pushed a glass of water and some pills into her hands.

'Painkillers—take them,' he ordered, and she

couldn't be bothered to argue. She needed them, anyway.

Jane came in and gasped, and Frankie heard Robert reassuring her. 'She's OK. She just needs to be quiet for a while. Why don't you go and watch telly in the drawing room, darling?'

The door closed, and Frankie felt her cheek tentatively. Lord, it was sore. She started to shake again.

'How's Jim?' she asked weakly, trying to take her mind off herself.

'He'll live. He's a bit battered. I'll ring later. Right, hold still; I'm going to put some ice on that bump.'

She flinched, and his face twisted with pain. 'I'm sorry,' he murmured. 'Just let me hold it there for a few minutes. It'll take the swelling down.'

He was as gentle as possible, but the ice hurt her almost more than the bruise, and whether from that or from reaction she wasn't sure, but tears welled in her eyes and she blinked them away.

'I'm sorry,' he said again, and his thumb brushed away the tears with such tenderness that they welled again.

'Just hold me,' she said brokenly, and, dropping the ice, he lifted her in his arms and carried her through into the sitting room, cradling her against his chest as he sat in his big old chair.

She slumped against him, too weary to fight the tears as he held her against his warmth and soothed her.

'What were you thinking about, going somewhere like that when it was getting dark?' he said crossly.

She sniffed. 'Don't be angry with me. I was worried.'

'You were worried?' His hand stroked her hair rhythmically as he scolded her, his voice raw with pain. 'My God, I thought you were going to die, Frankie. Have you any idea what it did to me, hearing you scream?' His arms tightened convulsively and he rested his head against hers, his chest heaving.

'I thought I'd lost you,' he whispered into her hair. 'I thought you'd die, and the whole of the rest of my life would be without you, knowing that I'd been too late— Oh, God, Frankie. . .'

His hand cradled the back of her head, and she felt a tear fall on her hand and realised with surprise that it was his.

'Robert? Darling, I'm all right,' she murmured. 'Don't cry for me—please; I'm fine now.'

He lifted his head and his eyes shone with tears. 'I never did tell you how much I love you, did I?' he whispered. 'I should have done. Even if we don't have a future, you ought to know that.'

The tears welled and he shut his eyes, sending them cascading down his cheeks. She brushed them away with trembling fingers.

'I love you too. Oh, Robert, what a mess. . .'

'How the hell am I going to live without you?' he asked quietly. 'Every night I lie and wonder where you are, what you're doing. I was going to come and see you, but I didn't think I could trust myself. I'm not very good with goodbyes.' He reached up and touched her bruised cheek with his gentle, loving fingertips, and his face twisted.

'He could have killed you,' he gritted. 'You might have died and never known how much I love you.'

Her heart was breaking. 'Robert, don't,' she pleaded, her tears threatening. 'I think I'd better go now. Take me back.'

'Frankie, I can't,' he said raggedly. 'Stay—please? Just until tomorrow? Let me make sure you're all right—'

'Dad?'

They both turned, startled, at the quiet sound of her voice.

'JJ,' Robert said, his voice reflecting his confusion.

'It's all right, Jane, I'm just going,' Frankie said quickly. 'I'm all right now—'

'You love her, don't you?' the girl carried on, her eyes fixed on Robert. 'It's not like Mum. She's all over them like a rash then drops them, but you're talking to Frankie like you do to me, angry with her because you were worried sick.'

She sniffed hard, tears spiking her lashes. 'You don't worry about people unless you love them, do you? Not really worry, so that you can't sleep at night. I know you don't sleep. I can hear you, walking about all night and playing music down here. . .'

She smudged the tears from her cheeks and looked at Frankie. 'Are you OK?' she asked in a whisper.

'Yes—I will be. I was just a bit scared, that's all. I'm fine now.'

'You were nearly killed,' Robert told her flatly. 'The guy in the suit had a knife with a six-inch blade. I think Gavin broke his wrist.'

'Good. He deserved it.' She gave a shudder and he squeezed her gently.

'Are you OK?'

She nodded. 'I am if I don't think about it.'

Jane crept closer, her eyes wide and serious. 'I heard Dad on the phone telling someone to call the police and saying he was just coming, and then I saw the way he drove off. I was really worried about you,' she quavered, and then the tears slid down her cheeks and Frankie held out her arm, gathering her onto Robert's lap too.

'It's a good job this is a big chair,' he said unevenly, and hugged his daughter close.

She burrowed into his shoulder, clinging to his neck, and over her head Frankie met his eyes and slid off his lap.

'I think you two need to talk,' she said softly. 'I'll put the kettle on.'

He smoothed Jane's hair back from her face as Frankie left the room and went through to the kitchen, pulling the door to behind her. She didn't shut it. She didn't feel quite that brave yet, not with the dark garden out there. She pulled down the blinds over the kitchen windows and put the kettle on, then huddled in the corner, arms wrapped round her aching ribs, and waited.

Had Jane changed her mind? Oh, dear God, please, she prayed. She couldn't live without him. She could understand now how her father could have killed himself rather than face life without his beloved wife. The past two weeks had been an endless wasteland, but she had thought he didn't love her so it had been easier to deal with.

Knowing now that Robert loved her would make it so much harder to walk away. . .

'You really do love her, don't you?'

Robert held his precious daughter carefully, and hoped to God he didn't blow this most important of conversations.

'Yes, I really do.'

'I didn't understand,' she said. 'I thought it was just—well, you know, just an affair. People have them all the time. I just thought you were different, and then finding out you were just the same was awful.'

He hugged her. 'I'm sorry about that. I would never in a million years have had you finding out like that. I was going to talk to you the next day, but you rather pre-empted that.'

She snuggled closer. 'What does "pre-empted" mean?'

He smiled slightly. 'It means you got there first.'

'Oh.' She shifted and looked at him, her young eyes wide. 'Is this a serious affair, Dad?'

He reached up and cupped her face, smoothing the soft, young skin lovingly. 'It's rather more than an affair, sweetheart. I love her very much—much more than I can say.'

'Are you going to marry her?'

Oh, God. He felt the ground shift beneath his feet, and trod cautiously. 'Would you mind?'

She looked worried. 'Would it change things? I mean, could I still come here for weekends occasionally?'

'*Occasionally*? Darling, this is your *home*,' he stressed. 'Of course you'd be here—every weekend, every holiday—always. Oh, JJ, we'd never shut you out, darling.'

'Mum does. When she meets somebody new she never wants me around.'

'Well, I do, and so does Frankie. She's very fond of you, Jane. She cares very much about you.'

'Really?' She looked surprised. 'Why should she care about me?'

He smiled tenderly at her. 'Because she loves me? Because you're part of me? Maybe, just maybe, because you're actually rather lovable.'

She blushed and punched his chest gently. 'Don't tease.'

'I'm not.' He hesitated, then took a deep breath. 'Jane?'

'Mmm?'

'About Frankie.'

'Mmm?'

'I really do want to marry her, but if you don't want me to, really feel it would hurt you if I did, then I won't.'

She looked at him in wonder. 'You'd do that for me?'

'Of course.'

'But you love her.'

'Yes, but I love you too.'

A slow smile crept onto her lips. 'I think she'd make a good mum, don't you?'

A huge knot of tension in his chest dissolved away, leaving him drained. 'Yes, I do. As a matter of fact, I think she'd make a wonderful mother.'

Jane ran her fingertip down his nose. 'Will you have more children?'

He laughed, unable to trap the happiness. 'I think I should ask her that. I haven't even asked her to marry me yet.'

She leapt off his lap instantly.

'Don't you think you should?'

He grinned at her and got to his feet. 'Yes, I do.'

He went to the door and opened it, then turned back to Jane. 'Stay here,' he ordered.

She saluted, a cheeky grin on her face, and with a wry chuckle he went in to Frankie.

As soon as she heard him laugh, she knew it was all right.

She stood up and held out her hands to him, and he wrapped his arms round her carefully and cradled her against his heart.

'Is she OK?' Frankie asked, just to be sure.

'She's fine. She wants to know if we'll have more children.'

Frankie eased away from him, her heart overflowing. 'Isn't there something missing?' she teased.

He gave a wry grunt of laughter. 'You're going to make me do it properly, aren't you?'

She nodded, the mischief dancing in her eyes, and with a resigned sigh he went down on one knee on the kitchen floor, took her hand in his and looked up into her eyes.

'Frances Bradley, I love you,' he said. 'You mean more to me than I could have believed possible, and without you my life just won't be complete.' He brushed his lips over the back of her hand, sending a shiver down her spine. Then he looked up at her again, and the look in his eyes made her heart soar and brought tears to her foolish eyes.

'Marry me, Frankie. Have my children, and let me look after you and love you till we're old and grey. Then you can do my hip replacements and I'll do yours, and we'll creak on till we're too old to do anything more than talk about the old times.'

He stood up and cupped her shoulders in his hands, drawing her near him as the smile faded. 'I want to grow old with you, Frankie. I want to watch our children grow, and their children, and their children's children—'

'We'd better start soon, then, hadn't we?' she said lightly, but her lip trembled and she buried her face in his neck and gave a little hiccuping sob.

'Frankie? Was that a yes?' he asked.

She nodded, and behind them Jane shrieked in delight.

'Yes!' she yelled, punching the air, and with a laugh Robert turned towards her.

'I thought I told you to stay out, minx,' he scolded lovingly.

'And miss that? No way! Think of all the blackmail potential! I should be able to drag Frankie off shopping for years on the strength of that!'

Robert laughed and hooked his arm round her neck, drawing her into their arms. 'Just promise me something?'

'What?'

'Don't teach your sisters how to shop? Please. . .?'

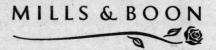

MILLS & BOON

MEDICAL ROMANCE

LOVE ON CALL

The books for enjoyment this month are:

AND DAUGHTER MAKES THREE	Caroline Anderson
A QUESTION OF TRUST	Maggie Kingsley
THE DISTURBING DR SHELDON	Elisabeth Scott
CONSULTANT CARE	Sharon Wirdnam

Treats in store!

Watch next month for the following absorbing stories:

BUSH DOCTOR'S BRIDE	Marion Lennox
FORGOTTEN PAIN	Josie Metcalfe
COUNTRY DOCTORS	Gill Sanderson
COURTING DR GROVES	Meredith Webber

Available from W.H. Smith, John Menzies, Volume One,
Forbuoys, Martins, Woolworths, Tesco, Asda, Safeway and
other paperback stockists.

Readers in South Africa - write to:
IBS, Private Bag X3010, Randburg 2125.

GET 4 BOOKS
AND A MYSTERY GIFT

Return this coupon and we'll send you 4 Love on Call novels and a mystery gift absolutely FREE! We'll even pay the postage and packing for you.

We're making you this offer to introduce you to the benefits of Reader Service: FREE home delivery of brand-new Love on Call novels, at least a month before they are available in the shops, FREE gifts and a monthly Newsletter packed with information.

Accepting these FREE books and gift places you under no obligation to buy, you may cancel at any time, even after receiving just your free shipment. Simply complete the coupon below and send it to:

MILLS & BOON READER SERVICE, FREEPOST, CROYDON, SURREY, CR9 3WZ.

No stamp needed

Yes, please send me 4 free Love on Call novels and a mystery gift. I understand that unless you hear from me, I will receive 4 superb new titles every month for just £2.10* each postage and packing free. I am under no obligation to purchase any books and I may cancel or suspend my subscription at any time, but the free books and gifts will be mine to keep in any case. (I am over 18 years of age)

1EP6D

Ms/Mrs/Miss/Mr _____

Address _____

_____

_____ Postcode _____